# TRUE HEROES
## OF
# GETTYSBURG

# TRUE HEROES
# OF
# GETTYSBURG

JOHN HINMAN

iUniverse, Inc.
Bloomington

# True Heroes of Gettysburg

*iUniverse books may be ordered through booksellers or by contacting:*

*iUniverse*
*1663 Liberty Drive*
*Bloomington, IN 47403*
*www.iuniverse.com*
*1-800-Authors (1-800-288-4677)*

*ISBN: 978-1-4620-3857-2 (sc)*
*ISBN: 978-1-4620-3858-9 (hc)*
*ISBN: 978-1-4620-3924-1 (ebk)*

*Printed in the United States of America*

*iUniverse rev. date: 8/08/2011*

# Chapter 1

## THE GREAT SNAKE CAPER

What is the best way to completely disrupt a classroom? The goal is not about creating a little disturbance, where the teacher's glare can put everything back in order again, but to create such a big disruption that it would be almost impossible for the teacher to stop it once it began. But how do you do it? How can you create so much confusion that a teacher cannot help but let all of the students go home early?

That was Darrell Stouffer's dilemma as he sat by the edge of the creek, eating his lunch at midday recess. Darrell was a tall, lanky thirteen-year-old. During the past year, he had sprouted up past his father in height to stand nearly six feet tall. His weight, however, did not increase as rapidly as his height, giving him a string-bean physique.

Darrell was a bright kid. He was by far the smartest student in the one-room Dubaville, Pennsylvania, schoolhouse. Darrell's passion was reading. He read anything he could get his hands on. Mrs. Garber, the Dubaville schoolteacher, had a large library of books, and Darrell had already read each one of them at least two or three times.

Darrell had a smart-alecky attitude that sometimes got him into trouble. He loved to be disruptive in school. He was considered to be the most challenging student in class by Mrs. Garber. Darrell, along with his best friend Kenny McElroy, had carried out some of the greatest pranks in Dubaville educational history. This was the last day of school before summer recess, May 15, 1863, and Darrell wanted to play one last great prank.

"It's almost time to go back inside, and I don't have any idea of what to do to have some fun," Darrell said to Kenny, who was sitting beside him.

"You'll think of something," Kenny answered. Kenny was more interested in eating his third sandwich than in helping to think up a good practical joke. Kenny was a big, stocky thirteen-year-old. He was the largest student in school—both in height and in weight. He was a little taller than Darrell, but Kenny was solidly built. Although he was strong, Kenny was quiet and gentle and always followed Darrell around.

Kenny had two loves in his life—food and farming. His mother always sent him to school with the biggest lunch pail, stuffed with as much food as she could find. Despite the fact that he had twice as much food as everyone else, Kenny was always the first one done, and then he would go around begging for food from the other students. As soon as Kenny got home from school, he would hurry out to help his father in the cornfield. Because he was so big, he did all of the chores that a grown man would undertake. Kenny loved farming with his father, and he knew that his future would be working with the soil.

Darrell looked over at his friend fondly. "I just gotta come up with something to do before we go back in," Darrell said. "It's gotta be bigger than anything we ever did before."

"Hey, Darrell," Kenny said. "Remember when we tied Reggie Saunders's shoelaces together and then we yelled '*Fire!*'? When he got up to run out of the room, he fell flat on his face. That was a real good one!"

"Yeah, but we did stuff much better than that one. My favorite was when we snuck into school at night and took out all the furniture. Remember? We hid everything behind Old Man Brinager's barn. I can still see Mrs. Garber's face when she came to school the next morning, and the only thing still there was the blackboard!"

"She was so mad. We spent the entire day moving everything back. That was fun!" exclaimed Kenny.

"Remember when we snuck out one night and caught all them frogs in the pond and dumped them in school? When everybody came the next day, them frogs were everywhere!"

"Yeah, the frogs jumped all over the place. They even jumped on some of the kids. Remember when one of them jumped on Mrs. Garber's dress, and she started screaming? I never laughed so hard in my life," Kenny said.

"It took us forever to get rid of all them frogs and clean up all of that mud that they brought in. And remember how bad that room stunk? We couldn't go back to school for almost a week until the place aired out! Now that's what I call a good prank," Darrell said. He enjoyed basking in the glory of his practical jokes.

It was more important to Darrell to have fun than it was to do just about anything else. As Benjamin Stouffer's oldest son, Darrell would one day inherit everything, including the farm and the Stouffer house. But Darrell didn't share Kenny's love of farming. He did his chores and helped his father, but he did it from a sense of duty, not from a desire to work the land.

Darrell's real interest was in the civil war that was being fought at the time between the Union and the Confederate armies. He followed the war closely in newspaper articles printed in the *Dubaville Times*. He wanted to join the army and be a great war hero with medals and parades in his honor, but his father refused to let him join because he was so young. So Darrell waited for the day when his father would let him enlist or when he was brave enough to run away. In the meantime, he would have as much fun at school as he could.

Darrell put his bare feet in the little creek that flowed by the school. In May, the water level was halfway up the creek's bank. The water flowed steadily and was clear and cold. By midsummer, the creek would almost completely dry up under the hot and nearly rainless Dubaville weather. Darrell splashed the water a little with his feet, and then he saw them: two small, light brown garter snakes that were making their way up the muddy bank of the creek. His mind raced, and he had an idea for the greatest caper that he had ever attempted.

"Quick! Kenny! Grab one of those snakes!" Darrell commanded.

Kenny reached over, and with one quick snatch, he was holding one of the garter snakes. Darrell now knew they were going to pull off another great stunt. Once he got that thought in his head, there was no stopping him. Darrell could see that Kenny was waiting in anticipation for him to explain the prank.

"These snakes'll be perfect for my plan, Kenny," Darrell said excitedly, grabbing the other snake.

"What're we gonna do with them—throw 'em down someone's shirt?" Kenny asked.

"Nah, Kenny, wait and see," Darrell said. "This'll be the best prank we've pulled off yet, but we need some help."

Darrell looked around and then yelled, "Hey, Timmy and Tommy! Come over here!"

Timmy and Tommy Martin were ten and eight years old, respectively. They were spoiled children, whose father always gave them anything that they wanted. The boys had the newest toys and the best clothing of anyone around. Timmy and Tommy were studious types, and they were also teacher's pets. They liked their roles as Mrs. Garber's favorites. Other students teased them for running behind Mrs. Garber and helping her in school, but the two boys didn't care.

Timmy was clumsy, tripping over almost everything in his path. He brought his lunch to school in a metal pail, which he often spilled onto the ground. To fix this problem, his father had Mr. Brinager devise a wooden lid for his pail. Even though Tommy wasn't as clumsy as his older brother, he had demanded that a lid be put on his lunch pail, too. Mr. Martin had complied. The two lunch pails with their lids were just what Darrell needed to sneak the snakes into school!

"Hey, lemme see your lunch pail," Darrell asked Tommy. "Does that lid stay on tight?"

Tommy responded, "Yeah, it stays good and tight."

Darrell held a prominent position in school. He was one of the oldest students, and he was always doing something fun. He had acquired a hero status among the younger students because of his pranks. That worship fed Darrell's need to play practical jokes and to disrupt the class.

"See these snakes?" Darrell asked. "You think they could fit in your lunch pails?" Darrell knew that they could, but he wanted the boys to feel like they were part of the planning.

"Sure they could!" little Timmy Martin exclaimed.

"I want you two to sneak these snakes into school. I'll tell you when to let 'em loose. Now don't go giggling and give this all away, you hear me?" Darrell commanded.

Being Mrs. Garber's favorites was one thing, but the great Darrell Stouffer had just asked them to be a part of one of his escapades. This made the two boys feel special, and they quickly turned their backs on their poor, unsuspecting teacher.

"What are we gonna do with the snakes, huh, Darrell?" Timmy asked.

"Just watch!" Darrell said as he and Kenny stuffed the snakes into the boys' lunch pails and closed the lids.

Darrell wasn't done. He needed more help if he was going to really turn the school upside down. He needed girls!

Timmy and Tommy had a younger sister named Tina. Tina was seven years old and every bit the teacher's pet that her older brothers were. But Tina had the loudest scream Darrell had ever heard. That was exactly what Darrell needed now. He called Tina to come over.

"Hey, Tina. Look inside Timmy's lunch pail," Darrell requested with a smile on his face. Timmy giggled and obliged by opening up his lunch pail lid.

When Tina saw the garter snake, she let out an ear-piercing screech. Most of the other students playing in the schoolyard stopped and looked at her. The Martin boys were laughing uproariously.

"Can you do that again in the classroom?" Darrell asked, excited about the volume of Tina's scream.

"You show me that snake again, and I'll yell even louder," Tina answered.

"How about jumping up on your bench to escape the snakes? You think you can do that?" Darrell was now laying out the entire plan.

"Sure. I can jump up and down if you want me to," Tina volunteered.

"You think you can get your friend Mary Lou Bolton to jump up and scream, too?" Darrell asked.

"Yeah, she'll do it. She hates snakes worse than me," Tina snickered.

"Don't go into class giggling like that. Mrs. Garber'll know something's up," Darrell ordered. "You three stay here with me and Kenny. We'll all walk in together."

Darrell thought for a moment. He needed one more thing to make his plan work. He had two girls who could scream, but he needed more. There were only two girls he could think of that would do the trick. He looked over at Kenny apologetically.

"Sorry to have to do this to you, Kenny, but I'm gonna need more help," he said. "Hey, Maggie, come over here."

"What do we need her for?" Kenny asked. "I don't wanna get near that thing."

Maggie Kirkpatrick was twelve years old, and she had a huge crush on Kenny. Some days she did nothing other than stare across the aisle of desks at him. Maggie had red, frizzy hair that she tried to braid, but it made her look like she had two big birds' nests attached to her head. She was a tall, stocky girl who liked eating just as much as Kenny did. Her friend Phoebe Johnson went everywhere Maggie did, and the two girls came over to Darrell as Maggie let out a flirtatious giggle.

"Do we really need Maggie?" Kenny pleaded.

"Yeah, she's important," Darrell replied with a little smile. "Maggie, I want you to look into Tommy's lunch pail. Tommy, show her what's inside."

When Tommy showed Maggie his garter snake, she simply grabbed it and laughed as it slithered in her hands. This was not the reaction Darrell was hoping for.

"You're not afraid of snakes?" Darrell asked.

"Nah," Maggie responded. "I think this one's cute."

"Can you be afraid of snakes?" Darrell asked.

"If you want me to be scared, I could be," Maggie said. "I can scream even louder than Tina can—*if somebody really wanted me to.* All you have to do is get that someone to ask me."

Darrell understood what Maggie was trying to do. She had found a way to get Kenny to do something with her. He felt sorry for his best friend, but when it came to planning pranks, personal feelings had to be put aside.

Darrell kicked Kenny in the shin. "Ask her, Kenny!" he pleaded.

"Will you scream at the snakes?" Kenny whispered, hardly audible.

"What?" Maggie said, giggling. She finally had Kenny where she wanted him.

"Will you scream when you see the snakes?" Kenny scowled and kicked at the dirt.

"I'll do it on one condition—you have to walk me home," Maggie replied.

"No way," Kenny said. "I don't want to get any of your germs!"

"Kenny, we really need Maggie's help," Darrell intervened. "Tell her you'll walk her home," and he pushed him toward Maggie.

Kenny was stuck. Darrell needed Maggie's help, and the only way to get it was for him to do something that he greatly detested, but there was no other choice. "Okay, I'll walk you home, but I ain't carrying your books or talking to you the whole way," Kenny said, feeling that at least he had salvaged something in the trade.

"And you got to get Phoebe Johnson to scream and jump up on her bench, too," Darrell bargained.

"I'll be waiting for you after school, Kenny," Maggie said as she and Phoebe giggled together.

The stage was set when Mrs. Garber rang the bell, signaling the end of lunch. With this, the small group of mischievous students moved their way excitedly toward school.

The Dubaville school's one room was composed of twenty desks, ten on each side with a small aisle separating the two sides. Instead of individual seats, the students sat two to a bench. The girls sat on the left side of the room, and the boys sat on the right. The youngest students sat up front, and the oldest students sat in the back of the room. Kenny and Darrell were in the last row of the boys' seats, and Maggie Kirkpatrick and her friend Phoebe sat behind all of the female students.

Mrs. Garber, the schoolteacher, was serious about her job—sometimes a little too serious. She carefully planned every minute of her classes, and she lost patience many times with Darrell and Kenny's disturbances. She was twenty-five years old but dressed as if she were at least twenty years older. Today, her dress was plain and drab, which made her tall, thin body look even thinner. Her blonde hair was pulled back tightly and tied into a bun. She was all business when she entered the school building.

Mrs. Garber loved reading to the students, and she was planning on reading the poem *The Song of Hiawatha* by Henry Wadsworth Longfellow. After the poem, she was going to have a little party and give her students the cookies that she had baked the previous evening. She explained her schedule to the students after they took their seats.

"Students, I want to read one of my favorite poems to you," Mrs. Garber pronounced excitedly to the class. "It is a newer poem written by a man named Henry Wadsworth Longfellow. Let me write the name of the poem and the author on the blackboard."

This was the break that Darrell was looking for. He could hardly have wished for a longer name of a poem and its poet. By the time Mrs. Garber had finished writing the names on the board, the snakes would be out of the lunch pails.

As the teacher turned her back to the students, Darrell put his plan into action. He nodded to Timmy and Tommy to release their snakes. Even the snakes seemed to know their part in the episode, because they slithered their way across the empty aisle toward the girls' side of the room.

Darrell looked at Tina Martin, and right on cue, she started screaming, "Snakes! Look out for the snakes!"

Tina and her friend Mary Lou began jumping up on their bench. Their screams made Mrs. Garber turn to face the class, but it was too late to do anything. Once a perfect prank gets started, a teacher is powerless to stop it.

"I'm afraid of snakes!" shouted Maggie, earning her escort home. Then she and her friend Phoebe started jumping on their bench, creating even more noise than Tina and Mary Lou had made.

The rest of the girls, either sensing that they could be a part of something fun or seeing the two snakes heading toward them, began screaming and jumping. The noise and the movement must have scared the snakes, because they turned around and went scurrying back toward the boys. Then it was the boys who were screaming and jumping on benches. The whole room was bedlam. Even if Mrs. Garber had wanted to say something, no one would've heard it.

Darrell gave Tina a nod. She jumped down from her bench, arms flailing, and she and Mary Lou went running out the door. These first escapees set off a flood of students, yelling and screaming and running around the schoolhouse. The benches were flying all over the place, kids were running into each other, and Mrs. Garber just stood there with her mouth wide open.

The excited students ran around the yard of the school. They were yelling and laughing, waiting for Darrell to tell them what to do next.

Darrell yelled out, "Let's get outta here!" At his signal, all of the students raced off in different directions. It took less than three minutes for Darrell to turn the whole school upside down and send students heading for home.

Darrell Stouffer had carried out his historic disruption of school—something that once it got started, it was impossible to stop.

Sarah Garber looked at her classroom: benches upturned, desks pushed in every direction, no student in sight. She sat down, put her face in her hands, and began to cry. Suddenly she felt something touch her foot. She looked down to find one of the garter snakes crawling over her shoe. The 1862-1863 school year was now officially over.

# Chapter 2

## THE TATTLETALE

Most families with more than one sibling usually have one child who provides the services of a tattletale. In the Stouffer family, that child was Jeremiah. Benjamin and Anna Stouffer had four children: Darrell was thirteen, Jacob was twelve, Jeremiah was nine, and Mary Ellen was seven. Jeremiah was his parents' eyes and ears when they were not around. Not only was he good at relaying each detail to his parents when anything went wrong, but he also took great joy in standing next to them with a smug grin on his face while they questioned the culprit.

Every time Darrell carried out one of his pranks at school, Jeremiah would inform his parents. "The Great Snake Incident," as it would later be called, gave Jeremiah something new to tattle on Darrell. Jeremiah had run ahead of the other Stouffer children as they traveled home from school. Darrell knew Jeremiah would have completely described the whole episode before Darrell even reached his front door. He also expected punishment to fall on him later that evening, what he deemed as small retribution for committing such a fun and clever crime.

Anna Stouffer was weeding in her garden when Jeremiah came running home. She had once been young and pretty, but as Anna reached her midthirties, she claimed she felt old after working hard her whole life. She attributed the lines on her face to dealing with the problems that Darrell kept causing.

"Hi, Mom!" Jeremiah yelled, barely able to hold back this latest tale of Darrell's misbehavior until he was at her side.

"Is it midafternoon already?" Mrs. Stouffer asked. "Where did all the time go? Seems like I just got out here to do some weeding."

"No, it ain't midafternoon. We're home from school early. You wanna know why?" Jeremiah announced as he got ready to go into the details of his story.

"Well, that was nice of Mrs. Garber to let you out early on the last day of school. Where's the rest of the clan?" Mrs. Stouffer requested.

"She didn't let us out early. We let ourselves out early, thanks to Darrell!" Jeremiah excitedly exclaimed.

"What do you mean you let yourselves out early? And what did Darrell do now?" his mother demanded as she stood up from her weeding and scowled at Jeremiah.

Jeremiah related the details of Darrell's caper. He enjoyed describing each part of the event with great detail. His mother grew angry at Jeremiah's story, and she shook her head in disbelief.

"That Darrell. Why does he like to torment that poor teacher so much? I swear he must have a backside made of iron, because it don't do no good for his father to whoop him. He keeps on doing the same old dumb things," Mrs. Stouffer lamented.

"I dunno why he's got to be so bad. Is Dad gonna take him back to the woodshed again? I think he deserves worse, don't you, Mom?" Jeremiah said. He was clearly enjoying his task.

The usual punishment for one of Darrell's pranks was a trip to the woodshed, where Benjamin Stouffer would have a freshly cut switch to paddle him with. But after so many trips out to the woodshed, Darrell's father grew tired of wasting his energy on his son's backside. It didn't do any good. Darrell would be back doing some other mischievous activity before he knew it. So he made the trips to the woodshed look good to get his wife off of his back, but he and Darrell spent more time talking than carrying out the punishment.

"Now you mind your own business, Jeremiah," Mrs. Stouffer scowled. "Your father and I will take care of the punishments. Go find your brother and bring him here to me."

Off went Jeremiah to find Darrell. Bringing in the wanted criminal was Jeremiah's favorite part of tattling. Darrell couldn't hit him for blabbing, because that would just earn him more punishment later on. Although his parents tried to tell Jeremiah that tattling on others was bad, he provided an invaluable service about the comings and goings of the other kids when they weren't around, and so they protected him from any repercussions.

"Hey, Darrell," Jeremiah smugly said to his brother when he ran back to get him. "Mom says she wants to see you right away. You're in big trouble now! She says Dad's gonna whoop you when he gets home." That last part was a lie, but Jeremiah thought it added such a nice touch.

"You wait, you little weasel. You'll go to sleep one night and never expect what I might do. Maybe I'll put a snake in your bed, and maybe it'll be a poisonous one."

"I'm telling Mom that you threatened me. You put anything in my bed, and you'll be sorry." With that, Jeremiah raced back to the protection of his mother.

Darrell learned early on that with a tattletale like Jeremiah, he had to own up to what he did and not try to lie to get out of it. Jeremiah would have already provided so many details that there was no way he could have made up his story. And so, Darrell always confessed to the wrongdoing right away to avoid further punishment for fibbing. There was nothing to be ashamed about. His latest escapade was better than anything he had ever done before.

*I'm famous*, he thought. *No other student will ever match my pranks.*

There was pride in his step. No matter what his mother and father did to him, they could not take away this feeling of triumph. He was the great Darrell Stouffer.

"You wanted to see me?" Darrell asked his mother innocently when he got home.

Darrell's mother was still weeding in the garden. The family garden was behind their house and provided Mrs. Stouffer with a place to escape the children while also taking care of the plants. The garden had beans, peppers, strawberries, and other fruits and vegetables that provided nourishment for the Stouffer family. Spending time in the garden was usually a peaceful time for her, but with Jeremiah's latest news, Mrs. Stouffer was anything but relaxed.

"Do you wanna explain to me what happened in school today?" Mrs. Stouffer demanded as she glared at her oldest son.

"Why should I? Jeremiah's probably already told you the whole thing. He's always running to you and snitching on the rest of us." Darrell thought that if he could turn this discussion into a debate about whether to tattle or not, his mother might forget about the real reason she wanted to see him.

"You leave your brother outta this. You're the one who's sneaking snakes into school. I swear, Darrell Anthony, I don't know where you got this devil in you, but that ole demon seems to take aim at poor Mrs. Garber. And she's always been nice to you. Why do you gotta be a thorn in her side?"

"I dunnos," was Darrell's answer. He learned a long time ago that it was better to keep on saying "I dunno" than to give a real answer. His mother hated that phrase, and so Darrell used it often. The more "I dunno's," the easier it would be to get the conversation to end quickly. If he gave his mother a real answer, he would have to listen to her lecture about why he had to be so bad.

"I hate it when you say that. I wish you would just come right out and give me an answer. You know, one day, Darrell Anthony Stouffer, you're gonna regret all the things that you did to Mrs. Garber."

Darrell had heard that line so many times before. Moms had to say things like that. How often did they ever come true? How would he ever regret doing anything to Mrs. Garber? And how could his mother know what it was like to be the hero at school? He was the star, couldn't she see that? The other students would remember one thing about today's class—how the great Darrell Stouffer brought down the school. What did his mother know about having a whole school look up to you?

"Well, you wait till your father gets in from the fields. He'll teach you to have more respect for your elders. Now, watch the rest of the children while I finish up out here in the garden. And you better leave Jeremiah alone, you hear me?"

"Yes'm," Darrell said as he made his way to round up his brothers and his sister.

This was one of Darrell's most hated jobs. Jacob and Jeremiah were always bickering with each other, leaving Darrell to be the referee. And Mary Ellen only wanted to play with her dolls.

Darrell brought the group to the side of the house so that he could play a game with his brothers while Mary Ellen sat by the house playing with her two favorite dolls. On the side of the house was a clearing bordered by a thick wooded area. The three boys usually played in the clearing, but on this day, Darrell dreamed up a new game that used both the woods and the clearing.

"Hey, Jacob and Jeremiah. Let's play war. You two are the Confederates, and I'm the Union army. Jacob, you're General Robert E. Lee. Jeremiah, you're his private."

"I don't wanna be a private. Why can't I be a general?" Jeremiah whined.

"You're too small to be a general. My name is General George Meade," Darrell said.

"Who's that?" Jacob asked.

"He's from Pennsylvania. I read all about him in the newspaper. I bet if Abe Lincoln would put him in charge of the Northern army, we wouldn't be losing so much."

"But you always say that nobody beats General Lee," Jacob said, proudly thinking of his role in the upcoming game.

"Well, get ready to lose today. You guys see these sticks? We'll use them as our rifles. Now, you two have to protect this clearing, and I will sneak up from the woods behind you. Okay, I'm gonna go into the woods. You two make sure Mary Ellen doesn't go anywhere."

"As long as she's got her dolls, she ain't going no place," Jacob answered as Darrell ran away.

Darrell took off into the woods. There was excitement in his step. He was going to prove that he would make a great soldier. Darrell circled back to where he was less than fifty feet from the clearing that was being guarded by Jacob and Jeremiah. He could hear them arguing ahead.

"I told you to watch over there, and I'll watch behind us, Jeremiah. I'm the general. You have to do what I say," Jacob complained.

"No, I wanna guard behind us," Jeremiah argued.

"You never do what I tell you to do," Jacob cried.

"Well, Darrell ain't gonna come from over there. You just want me to get shot first. I'm gonna tell Mom that you keep bossing me around," Jeremiah whined.

Darrell knew that as long as they were fighting with each other he could keep sneaking closer to their protected ground. He decided that he needed something to divert their attention so that he could emerge from the woods unnoticed. Darrell looked to his left, and he saw a small, tan-colored rabbit. The animal couldn't have been two pounds in weight; it was very small. It was looking at Darrell with big, brown eyes, waiting for Darrell to make a move so that it could sprint away in the opposite direction. Darrell threw a little pebble at the rabbit, and off it ran, dashing out of the woods past Jacob and Jeremiah. As the two boys watched the rabbit fly by, Darrell came out of the woods with his pretend rifle blaring.

"Bang! Bang! I shot you both! You're dead, General Lee! That's what you get for coming up against the great General Meade! I win!" Darrell boasted.

"That wasn't fair," cried Jeremiah. "We wasn't ready."

"That's why I'm such a great soldier. I knew that you'd be watching that rabbit instead of looking for me!" Darrell proclaimed.

Jacob and Jeremiah began arguing over who should have been watching for Darrell. As for the victor of the "Battle of Stouffer Farm," Darrell stood proudly in the clearing. He was the hero at school with his great prank with the snakes, and now he was the heroic soldier who had just defeated General Lee and the pretend rebels!

# Chapter 3

## MRS. GARBER'S VISIT

Sarah Garber strongly believed in education. She knew most, if not all, of her students would someday become farmers or get married to a farmer. She still believed that her students should stay in school as long as they could and learn as much as possible. She also hoped that one of her students would go further than her small school and get a college education—and perhaps go on to a career as a politician or a doctor or a businessman.

Mrs. Garber looked at Darrell Stouffer as one student who could do this. He was extremely bright, loved to read almost as much as she did, and had natural leadership ability. The problem with Darrell was his constant ambition to be the class clown and to play practical jokes. But because she wanted to believe that Darrell would one day advance his education to the college level, she kept taking him back to school after every one of his childish practical jokes.

Then came Darrell's latest prank. Sarah Garber was upset when she returned home. The snake incident earlier in the day had ruined her end-of-the-year plans. Her husband, Samuel Garber, had had enough. He was tired of seeing his wife come home from school upset about Darrell's antics.

After a short conversation, Sarah knew what she had to do. It was time to make sure that neither Kenny nor Darrell would reenter school. She decided to pay a visit to both households to let the parents know about her decision.

Samuel told his wife that he would go with her to make sure that she didn't change her mind. At first Sarah was against her husband coming, but she saw that he wouldn't take no for an answer. So Sarah and Samuel Garber hitched a couple of horses to their wagon and went to visit both boys' homes. They visited the McElroy home first, and then they headed toward the Stouffer residence.

Dinner that evening at the Stouffers' was not a happy experience. Mrs. Stouffer had prepared a hearty meal with a roast and potatoes and fresh vegetables, but the news of Darrell's latest prank had left both parents angry. Darrell was mad at Jeremiah for telling on him, and Jacob was pouting over having lost in Darrell's war game. Not even Mrs. Stouffer's apple pie could liven up the situation.

Just as the family was finishing dinner and the boys were clearing the table, Jeremiah spotted a wagon coming up the path to their house.

"Hey, everyone! Mrs. Garber is coming, and Mr. Garber is with her!" Jeremiah yelled excitedly. "And I think I see a really big paddle with Mr. Garber. Darrell, if I was you, I'd run and hide!" Jeremiah lied about the paddle to make his brother squirm.

"Now, Jeremiah, you better quit teasing your brother, or you're gonna get it," Mrs. Stouffer warned. "Jacob, take your brother and sister outside while we're talking. Darrell, cut two pieces of pie for the company and set them out for 'em."

The meeting caught Darrell by surprise. Maybe this time he had finally gone too far. Couldn't anyone take a joke anymore? He was just having a little fun. Mrs. Garber had planned to let everyone out of school in a few hours anyway. He was just speeding up that process a little. Now his teacher and her husband were going to come and yell at him, and to make matters worse, he had to serve them dessert while they were yelling.

The Garbers came into the house and were greeted by Anna Stouffer.

"Sarah, how nice it is to have you visit," she said. "I really love the color of the dress that you are wearing. And Samuel, how's everything on your farm?"

"Fine," Samuel Garber said gruffly.

Darrell was mad that his mother was being so nice to the Garbers. He knew that they hadn't come for pleasantries, and he was nervous about the point of their visit. Surely his father would protect him if Mr. Garber wanted to whoop him. He was happy to see that Jeremiah's spotting of a paddle carried by Mr. Garber was a lie. He would have to get even with Jeremiah later.

Everyone sat down around the kitchen table. There were five people in all—Mr. and Mrs. Garber, Mr. and Mrs. Stouffer, and Darrell. Mr. Stouffer looked about as happy to be a part of this incident as Darrell was. He knew that he should be involved, but he also knew that it was better to keep his mouth shut and let his wife run the show.

"Before we start, Darrell has something that he wants to say, *don't you, Darrell?*" Mrs. Stouffer emphasized.

Darrell thought for a minute. What he really wanted to say was *no* and be a wise guy. He also knew that if he took that route, he would be making his mother even madder than she was. So he decided to give his mother what she really wanted—an apology to Mrs. Garber.

"I'm sorry for what happened at school today," Darrell said, barely audible to the group.

"Darrell, I just don't understand you," Sarah Garber lamented. "One day you're my biggest helper, and then the next day you're my biggest problem. Why do you insist on disrupting my class?"

"I dunno," Darrell mumbled. Maybe the "dunno" could help end this tortuous conversation. He looked at his mother, and she was fuming.

"I'm tired of you using that word for an excuse. Now you tell Mrs. Garber why you are always upsetting her class!" Mrs. Stouffer said.

"Do you have something against me, Darrell? Is it that you don't like me?" Mrs. Garber asked.

"No, Mrs. Garber. I think you're a fine teacher. I've learned a lot from you. Sometimes these stupid ideas pop into my head.

When I get 'em, I just gotta act on 'em. I guess I don't think it through."

"For a boy who has all the smarts that Darrell has, there's lots of times he don't think. I swear that boy will drive me to an early grave," Mrs. Stouffer said. It was hard for her to keep apologizing for her son every time he pulled another practical joke.

"If it was just you acting on them, it would be one thing," Mrs. Garber explained. "But today you got others involved in your practical joke. Part of my job is to teach my students to be good citizens. Today you taught the Martin kids that being bad in school was acceptable. I'm going to have to go back in the fall and try to undo that."

"Well, maybe I could come back in the fall and be your helper. I could help you teach the kids that it is wrong to misbehave," Darrell said. He didn't really mean what he had just said; he was just trying make amends in his mother's eyes by volunteering to make things turn out right.

When Darrell suggested that he should come back to school, Mr. Garber's head snapped to attention. He had come with his wife to make sure that she did not lose her courage and take either of the boys back in the fall. Just the hint that Darrell wanted to come back to school had him ready to act. Before he could say anything, though, Sarah spoke determinedly to Darrell.

"Darrell, you've learned so much at school. I'm really proud of what a good reader you've become. But I think today's little prank was enough. I think that it's time that you move on in your life. If you try to come back to school in the fall, you will not be welcome," Mrs. Garber said.

"I think you're right," Benjamin Stouffer spoke up. The fact that Mr. Stouffer said anything at all was a surprise. He was always seen and rarely heard. He always let his wife do his talking for him. He was suddenly taking part in this discussion, and his wife looked at him in wonder.

"I want to thank you kindly for all the learning you gave my boy and for working with my other young'uns, too," Mr. Stouffer continued. "But I think Darrell don't need you as his teacher anymore—I think he needs me to do the teaching. Starting tomorrow, I'll be learning him how to run the farm. You don't have to worry 'bout him going back to school in the fall."

Darrell listened to his father talk. Being the oldest son in the family, he knew that he would one day take over the running of the farm. His father's statement was a confirmation of this. Darrell didn't know what to think. He had hoped to be a great soldier. He had also hoped that he would do something other than farming. He didn't hate farming—he just didn't like it the way that his friend Kenny did. He thought if he went to school long enough he would figure out what he really wanted to be. Mrs. Garber had made it clear that he was done with school, and his father had made it clear that his future was on the farm.

The meeting was over. Everyone stood up, and the Garbers thanked Mrs. Stouffer for the pie. Mrs. Garber commented about how happy she would be to see the rest of the Stouffer children at school in the fall.

Darrell watched the Garbers as they left. Jeremiah ran over to say something to Mrs. Garber as she climbed into the wagon. Mrs. Garber laughed, and then off she and her husband went down the long path that led to the dirt road.

Darrell felt a tightening in his chest. There was a feeling he tried to understand.

*I never got a chance to figure out what I wanted to be in life,* he thought to himself. *Now I'm stuck here, and tomorrow I got to learn how to run a farm. Is that what I'm supposed to be—a farmer? Is Dubaville the only place I'll ever go? Do I give up my dreams of being a great soldier in the army because I'm needed here on the farm?*

Earlier in the day, he had felt like a great hero. Now, as Darrell watched his teacher depart, he felt he was watching his dreams of the future disappear.

# Chapter 4

## LIFE ON THE FARM

In the five weeks after Mrs. Garber's visit, Darrell began to learn how to run the family farm. He worked ten to twelve hours every day. He and his father had to plow the field, plant the corn, and then tend to the field by irrigating it. His father had decided that since he had full-time help, he would clear some of the woods beside his house so that he could plant more corn in the following year. This was harder work than Darrell ever had to do before.

Mr. Stouffer was taking his son to the woods to work on the day's project.

"C'mon, son," he said. "Today we have to clear some of the tree stumps. It's gonna take a lot of digging. Once we get the tree stumps a little loose, we'll use the horses to help us pull them out. Dig the whole way 'round the trunk, okay?"

"Dad, why do we need more land to plant corn?" Darrell whined. "We've been doing just fine with the crop that we've always raised."

"It'll be nice to have some extra money for the house. Next year, I'll take care of the old field, and I'll let you grow corn on the new one. We'll bring in twice as much money."

"But it's gonna take me hours to dig out this old tree stump."

"Good. Then I ain't gonna hear you complain for a while. Get busy, and I'll come back and check with you later."

Darrell looked up toward the house where Jacob and Jeremiah were playing a game. He wished that he was up there with his brothers. He wanted to have fun instead of working hard and sweating all day. He hadn't even been able to go next door to the McElroy farm to see Kenny in over a week. Maybe the Great Snake Incident wasn't so great after all. It had led to his training into the life of a farmer.

After digging around a tree stump for a while, Darrell looked down at his hands. His blisters were growing blisters. He wished that he were anywhere except in the woods digging around this big tree trunk.

He wished that he were a soldier in the war that was being fought somewhere down South. He remembered back to 1861 when Abraham Lincoln had called for volunteers to enlist in the army. Fifteen young men from the surrounding area had gotten together and decided to enlist. Darrell had wanted to join the group, but he needed his father's approval. He remembered their conversation.

"Dad?" Darrell had asked his father. "I want to join the other boys and go off to Harrisburg to enlist."

"Are you crazy?" his father answered. "You're only eleven years old. The United States Army does not recruit eleven-year-old boys."

"But I'm just as good a shot as most of those boys who are heading out," Darrell pleaded. "Look at ole Jason Crittendon. He's the worst shot of anyone in the entire state. He couldn't hit the broad side of a barn standing five feet away from it."

"Jason Crittendon is nineteen years old. He may be the worst shooter around, but he's sure old enough to join the army."

"Dad, you ain't being fair. How old you are shouldn't matter if you really want to be a soldier, and I really wanna be one."

"Darrell, I ain't gonna tell you no again. Now quit your bellyaching before I give you something to complain about."

If his father had let him go join the army two years ago, he wouldn't be out in the field digging up this stubborn stump. The stump had to be at least two feet around. Darrell tried digging around it to see if it would budge, but no matter how deep he dug, the tree trunk remained solidly in the ground. It was going to take the rest of the day to dig it out to a point where one of the horses could be used to drag it from its home in the ground. Thoughts of the war became a distant memory.

Darrell continued his labors in the field for the rest of the week. Then came Sunday. Darrell appreciated Sunday more than he ever had before. Sunday was a day of rest. No working in the fields.

Mrs. Stouffer began the day by preparing a big breakfast for the family. After the meal, she got everyone moving so that they could get to church on time. Darrell liked going to church in town. It was a chance to see all of his friends in one place. He was sure to see Kenny there. After everyone got dressed in their Sunday best, they piled into the wagon for the two-mile journey into town.

Dubaville was a small village of less than three hundred residents. Most of the citizens were farmers who lived on the many farms outside the town. Corn was the main crop grown in the area. After the harvest, farmers took their corn about fifteen miles away to Gettysburg, where it was sold as food for livestock.

On Sunday, almost 100 percent of the residents could be found attending church services at the Dubaville Methodist Church. The Stouffer's wagon entered the town on the north end and had to travel through Dubaville to get to the church located on its south end. Most of the businesses were found on Dubaville's one main road, and residents lived on the few side streets of the town.

"Dad, I think we've got the best town in the whole country!" Jeremiah exclaimed. "All of the businesses are painted red, white, and blue."

"Jeremiah," Darrell said to his brother, "you see the same buildings each week and make the same dumb remark. It's not like they just painted them. They've been this way for two years."

"Dad, Darrell said I was dumb. I'm not dumb," Jeremiah cried.

"I didn't say that you were dumb. I said what you said was dumb," Darrell answered.

"Jeremiah and Darrell! Quit your fighting. We're going to church. You need to settle down before we get there," Mr. Stouffer refereed.

"I remember when everybody painted the businesses," Jacob said. "It was before the big parade."

"The paint looks like it's fading," Darrell pointed out to his father. "Isn't it a little soon for paint to wash out like that?"

"Most people were in too much of a hurry to do the job right," his father said. "They just splashed on the paint real quick. The sun's been working on it these past two years."

Back in 1861, fifteen Dubaville boys were going to war, and the town wanted to send them off with a big parade. The businesses painted their storefronts to show their support. As the Dubaville boys paraded through town, heading off to Harrisburg to enlist, people wished them well and gave them food to eat along the way. The townspeople proudly told them that the war would be over soon now that the Dubaville boys were in it.

Darrell remembered how much his heart ached, watching that parade. He had wanted to be a part of it so badly. Because his father had kept him from joining the group, he wouldn't talk to him for a week after the parade. Benjamin Stouffer didn't care and enjoyed the respite from Darrell's whining during his period of silence.

After the parade, the people in town were excited, awaiting the one big battle that they believed would win the war. The people of Dubaville believed that after the Confederates experienced a sound defeat in such a battle, the South would come running back to join the United States.

The problem was that the North lost that first big battle. When the story of the first battle of Bull Run was recorded in the *Dubaville Times*, Darrell remembered the shock that many of the people showed. He heard their conversations: they couldn't believe that their mighty army had been defeated. In the next copy of the *Dubaville Times*, there was a story that stated that nine of the fifteen Dubaville boys were killed in the battle. Jason Crittendon was one of the dead. Darrell remembered how bad he felt because he had made fun of Jason earlier. As the war dragged on over the past two years, the people in town lost their excitement for it. To Darrell, the storefronts' faded paint was a lot like the businessmen's faded enthusiasm for the war.

By the time the Stouffers' wagon pulled up to the church, many of the local residents were already gathered outside its front door. Darrell saw his friend Kenny and jumped out of the wagon to say hello.

"Kenny, how are you doing?" Darrell asked.

"Okay," he answered. "I haven't seen you in a long time. What've you been doing over there on your farm?"

"My dad's been making me clear some land to plant more corn next year. I swear, if I don't find something fun to do soon, I'll die. Let's get together this afternoon. I'll think up something to do," he said, hoping to create some excitement.

"I wish I could. I've got relatives in from out of town. Mom says I gotta stick around and entertain them. They ain't going until tomorrow morning. I gotta stay home today," Kenny said. "I sure could use something fun to do though."

"Can't you tell your mother that I don't get much of a chance to do anything with you anymore? We work hard all week; we should at least be able to do something together on Sunday," Darrell pleaded.

"You try to tell her. I've been trying to get out of doing anything with my cousins for the past two days."

"Come on, boys," Mr. Stouffer called to Darrell and Kenny. "It's time to go inside for the service."

The Dubaville Methodist Church was a big, white-painted, wooden structure. Its insides were simply decorated, like the town that it served. There were just enough pews to hold its congregation. In the summer, the building was extremely hot when all of the people entered. There were only a few windows to help cool the place off.

Reverend Henesy, the town's minister, was prone to giving long sermons. He used to talk about the evils of the slavery practiced by the Southern states. Then he talked of the honor of the soldiers fighting to make their country whole again. But after so many losses, mostly due to the efforts of the Confederate general Robert E. Lee, Reverend Henesy talked of more biblical topics, such as avoiding sin. His sermons ran as long as sixty minutes. After the service, the congregation gathered outside the church to talk before going home.

Martin Clancy, a neighbor of the Stouffers, came over to greet them. "Hey, Darrell, here you go." He handed Darrell the latest copy of the *Dubaville Times*. Martin Clancy bought the newspaper, and when he was done reading it, he always brought it over and gave it to Darrell.

"There ain't much in there about the war," he said. "No one seems to know what happened to Bobby Lee and his army. They think he's coming north again."

"I wonder if he'd ever come to Pennsylvania?" Darrell asked Mr. Clancy.

"I doubt he'd come this far. Last time he came north he only made it to Maryland before turning around and heading back to Virginia," he said to Darrell. "There is one new thing about the war in the paper though."

"What's that?" Darrell asked.

"It seems that ole Abe Lincoln is gonna get rid of the latest general who couldn't beat Bobby Lee. The paper says that General Hooker is about to get fired," Mr. Clancy told Darrell.

"Did you hear that, Dad," Darrell said excitedly. "Mr. Clancy said that the paper has an article that says General Hooker is gonna get replaced."

"That's big news?" Mr. Stouffer asked. "Seems like every other month he's replacing a general. That's why the South's winning. They stay with the same guy—Bobby Lee." Benjamin Stouffer didn't have the same interest in the war that his son had. "Thank you, as always, for the newspaper, Martin. Darrell, it's time we get home. Say good-bye."

By the time he climbed into the wagon, Darrell had already read the articles about the war. On the way home, he would peruse them a second and third time. He studied the Dubaville newspaper like students studied notes for a test. If he ever went to war, he wanted to know everything about the generals and the battles that he could possibly know.

Sunday afternoon was a lazy time at the Stouffer residence. Anna Stouffer sat in a wooden rocking chair on the front porch of the house, knitting a sweater for Darrell to wear in the fields when the weather got colder. Benjamin Stouffer sat in a wooden high-back chair, whittling a stick of wood with his knife. He would trim the stick down to nothing and then grab another stick of wood and repeat the process. Darrell had been sitting on the porch rereading the newspaper. He now looked out over the front yard, trying to come up with an idea for something fun to do.

He turned to his father and asked, "Hey, Dad. Can I go into town and talk to Terry McIntyre?"

"On a Sunday?" his father answered. "Can't you leave that boy alone?"

"He says he likes it when I visit him." Darrell pleaded, "C'mon, Dad. I promise I won't stay long."

"Be home in time for supper," Mr. Stouffer ordered.

"I will!" Darrell yelled as he ran down the path to the dirt road to town.

Terry McIntyre was one of the Dubaville boys who went off to war in 1861. Terry fought two battles at Bull Run in Virginia, and he fought against the great Confederate general, Stonewall Jackson, in his Shenandoah Valley campaign.

Terry was injured at the battle of Antietam. He was taken to a field hospital where his right leg was amputated five inches above the knee. When he returned home to Dubaville everyone treated him like a hero. But when Terry went back to his farm, he realized that there was nothing he could do to run it. He had a wife and a small child, and he didn't know how he would take care of them. Every day, people from town brought food to the McIntyre residence. For a few months, Terry was rarely seen in town; he was depressed about his physical appearance.

Then his father talked him into selling his farm and moving into town. He got a room at the Dubaville Hotel. The owner, Horace Sprague, didn't have the heart to charge him any rent. Dan Wheeler, who owned the general store in Dubaville, hired Terry to work in his business. He didn't really need Terry's help, and Terry couldn't do very much, but Dan believed that he should help out the McIntyres, seeing that Terry's handicap came from fighting for his country.

So Terry mostly sat around all day telling stories about his experiences in the war to anyone who cared to listen to them. Darrell was his biggest fan. He had heard all of Terry's stories several times, but he still wanted Terry to tell them again and again.

Darrell found Terry sitting in a chair on the front porch of the hotel. He had a tall glass of ice tea on a small table next to him.

"Hey, Terry!" he yelled from a few feet away.

"How are you doing, Darrell?" Terry answered. "What brings you to town on a hot day like this?"

"I came to talk with you," Darrell said excitedly. "How's things going?"

"About the same. You know Dubaville—not a lot of excitement around here."

Darrell took a seat next to Terry. "Hey, guess what? No one can find out where General Lee is—or where his army is heading. You think he's going back to Maryland again?"

"I don't follow what's going on in the war that much anymore," Terry said. "I had enough of it after Antietam. I don't care where Robert E. Lee is going."

There was an awkward moment as Darrell struggled to think of what to talk about next. He looked down at the stub that was Terry McIntyre's right leg. His pants leg was pinned back behind his thigh.

Terry saw that Darrell was looking at his injured leg and said, "Did I ever tell you the story about how I got shot?"

"Yeah, but tell it again," Darrell said, happy to be talking about something Terry wanted to talk about.

"We was attacking early in the morning on this farm near Sharpsburg, Maryland. The rain had just stopped, and there was a little fog. Ole General Hooker thought it was a good time to move under the cover of the fog."

"Were you scared, Terry?" Darrell asked.

"The moment before you start firing is the worst. Then, when you're fighting, you don't got any time to think about how you feel."

"What happened next, Terry?" Darrell asked, even though he knew the answer.

"We surprised Stonewall's brigade. We came a-firing at him as we raced into a cornfield," Terry said. "The bullets were flying back and forth so thick that they cut down just about the whole crop. We was winning at first, but then old Stonewall's men got reinforced, and we were the ones running."

"Did you shoot any rebels, Terry?" Darrell asked.

"I don't know if I hit anyone. The rows of corn were too thick to see through. I just aimed at where the noise was coming from and shot. When we was moving back out of the cornfield, that's when I got hit."

"Did it hurt real bad?"

"Of course it did," Terry said. "The bullet tore half my leg off. I tried to get up, but I couldn't. I just had to lie there until someone helped me."

"When did they come for you, huh, Terry?" Darrell asked as the excitement of the story grew.

"It wasn't until the next day," Terry answered. "I just lay there all night, listening to other soldiers crying out in pain. I thought I'd bleed to death before anyone found me. The only thing that I could think about was how would my wife and kid get along without me."

"Did you like fighting in the army?" Darrell asked.

"I hated it. Once the firing started, I never knew if I'd come through the battle alive," Terry said.

"I bet I would make a good soldier," Darrell said.

"Listen, Darrell. You don't wanna go running off and joining the army," Terry said. "War is ugly. I've seen too much suffering and dying. Be thankful that you're too young to join up."

"But, Terry, I know I could come home a big war hero," Darrell said.

"Do you know how many of us Dubaville boys are still fighting?" Terry asked angrily. "There's only three left outta fifteen. I'm one of the lucky ones. Ten of us are dead. Dean Mulligan is still in a hospital in Washington. I hear that he's so bad that he'll never get released. No, Darrell, you just stick around Dubaville. If the war's still going on when you're eighteen, then maybe you can think about joining up."

"I better get going, Terry," Darrell said, wanting to end the conversation. He had hoped Terry would be on his side for enlisting in the army, but he was on his father's side—against him joining up.

"Hey, Darrell, thanks for stopping by," Terry said with sincere gratitude.

"I'm real busy on the farm, but maybe I can break away one day this week. I'll come and see you at the store," Darrell promised.

"I'd like that a lot," Terry smiled. "I'll be looking for you."

Off Darrell ran to get back home before dinner was ready. He raced through town, and on the other side he came to a grassy hill. The land rose up about thirty feet. The grass was tall, a light brown color from the latest dry spell.

Suddenly he was no longer Darrell Stouffer, farmer's son. He was Captain Stouffer of the Union army. He was looking over his company of two hundred soldiers. They were eagerly awaiting his orders.

"Boys, we're gonna have to take this hill from the rebs," he ordered to his make-believe army. "The fighting's gonna get tough, but follow my charge!"

On top of the hill was a group of angry, determined Confederate soldiers. Their guns were aimed at Stouffer's men, waiting for the attack to begin.

"All right, boys!" Darrell ordered his pretend soldiers. "Charge!"

Darrell began running up the side of the hill. Bullets were flying all around him, digging up the dirt as they exploded into it. But the brave captain showed no fear. The pretend Confederates at the top of the hill kept firing at the charging enemy; some of Stouffer's men went down, but Darrell was courageous as he led the assault. As his group got close to the top of the hill, the Confederates became frightened and ran in retreat.

Darrell was the first to reach the summit. His men gathered around him, shouting words of congratulations. They yelled that he might be the youngest officer in the Union army, but he sure was the bravest.

# Chapter 5

## THE MAKING OF THE PLAN

Monday was back to work as usual. Darrell's day started off by milking the cow and gathering the eggs from the hens. After breakfast, he went out to the fields. It was only morning, but the heat and the humidity were already assuring him that this was going to be a hard day of work.

"Darrell, we got to work to get more of the woods cleared," Mr. Stouffer told his son. "I sold the wood to McBride's Lumberyard. If we cut down the trees, he'll come over and haul the logs away. We need to cut down a lot of trees today."

"Dad, it's so hot. What if we took the day off and waited for when the weather got a little cooler?" Darrell moaned, trying to get out of work.

"If we wait till it gets cooler, them trees'll still be standing there in September. We'll take it a little slower, but we gotta cut down those trees."

"But after we cut down the trees, I'll have more stumps to remove," Darrell said.

"It'll keep you busy. We're already making money off of this new field by selling the wood to Mr. McBride. Just think how much we'll make next year when you plant corn on it."

Darrell was mad that all his father could think about was farming and making more money. Being a thirteen-year-old boy and having fun were not things that his father was willing to consider. With a saw and an ax, Darrell reluctantly headed to the woods to chop down trees. At one time this had been the scene of his great war victory over his brothers. Now it was a place of torturous work.

In less than a half an hour, his shirt was so soaked with sweat that he took it off. By midmorning, he was close to exhaustion. His mother came by with a glass of cool water just as Darrell thought that he would collapse from working in the heat.

"Benjamin!" Mrs. Stouffer exclaimed. "Ain't you working this boy too hard?"

"He'll be all right—especially if you don't baby him," Darrell's father said. "He's got to get used to working in the summer heat."

"But can't he take a little break? Look at him. He looks as if he's ready to fall over."

"Okay. He can rest for a little while, but I need him back to clear out more of the woods," Mr. Stouffer relented. He knew better than to get into an argument with his wife. She always got her way.

Darrell and his mother walked to the front of the house. He was glad to be taking a break from chopping down trees. Darrell collapsed in a chair on the front porch as his mother brought him a second glass of water. He was hot, his muscles ached, and he knew that at some point his father would be back to make him work in the woods again.

Just as he was coming back to life, Darrell saw Martin Clancy running up the dirt path to their house from the road. As usual, a copy of the newspaper was rolled up in his hands. Mr. Clancy owned the farm to the right of the Stouffer residence. He lived there by himself. His house was falling down, and his farm was in just as bad of shape. He only grew enough food to feed himself. Mr. Clancy spent most days looking around trying to find someone to talk to. He usually went into town to find an audience, but seeing Darrell on the front porch, he realized that he didn't have to walk that far. Mr. Clancy looked excited as he hurried up to the Stouffer porch.

"They found 'em, Darrell," Mr. Clancy said, almost out of breath from running.

"Hi, Mr. Clancy. What are you talking about? Who'd they find?" Darrell asked.

"Bob . . . bie Lee," Mr. Clancy said between puffs of breath. "The article in the newspaper said that they found Bobby Lee and the Confederate army."

"It did!" exclaimed Darrell as he began to catch Mr. Clancy's excitement. "Where does it say that they are? Are they in Maryland again?"

"No, they're closer than that. They're in Pennsylvania. One person in the article said he spotted some rebs not twenty miles away from here! You wanna know where the paper says that they think they're going?" Mr. Clancy enjoyed telling stories by only giving out little bits of information at a time.

"Are they coming to Dubaville?" Darrell asked, hoping that the war would come close to home so that he could fight in it.

"Dubaville? Why would Bobby Lee wanna come here? No, the newspaper says that the rebs are going to Harrisburg."

"Harrisburg is still less than sixty miles away, Mr. Clancy. Where's our boys?" Darrell asked.

"They're right behind Bobby Lee and closing in faster and faster, the newspaper said. You wanna know what else it says about our army?"

"Yeah, what's in there?"

"Well, remember yesterday I told you that the paper said that Abe Lincoln was thinking of getting rid of General Hooker as head of the army?"

"Yeah, I remember. Did he do it?" Darrell asked, frustrated that Mr. Clancy took so long to tell him anything.

"Yep. He fired him. Put some general named Meade in charge."

"I heard of General Meade," Darrell said. "There was a big article about him in the *Dubaville Times* after the battle of Chancellorsville. He's from Pennsylvania!"

"Yep. I think Lincoln's finally got some smarts, putting a Pennsylvania guy in charge—especially with Lee in his home state. Them rebs are in for it now."

"Mr. Clancy, that's great news, but everybody Lincoln puts in charge swears they're gonna beat Bobby Lee, and nobody's been able to do it."

"Well, if you keep switching leaders long enough, you're bound to hit on a good one every now and then. Maybe this one's a good one," Mr. Clancy said, finally finished with telling all of the news in the newspaper article.

"Can I read the paper, Mr. Clancy?" Darrell asked. He was excited to read about all of the things that Mr. Clancy had talked about.

"Yeah, sure. I'm heading into town. A lot of the old-timers'll be at Hawkins's Barbershop talking. I gotta get down there. Wanna come with me?"

"Nah, my father's got me cutting down trees in the woods by the house. He wants to clear the land to plant more corn."

"Cutting down trees in this heat? That's mighty tough work. I'd wait for it to cool off."

"That's what I told him," Darrell said. He was happy to have someone on his side for once. "But you know my father—sunup to sundown."

"Well, here's the newspaper. Have fun reading about the war. I gotta go before they talk about all of the good topics."

"Thanks, Mr. Clancy. Hey, if you're going by Wheelers, can you say hi to Terry McIntyre for me?"

"Sure. Have fun cutting down trees," Mr. Clancy said as he began running down the path to hurry to town.

Darrell read the paper, and he got all excited. Everything that Mr. Clancy had talked about was in there. The Confederate army was in Pennsylvania and was thought to be heading to Harrisburg. The local residents of the city were in a panic. Darrell read the article again. Then he stopped—suddenly, he had a plan.

Over the past two years he had bugged his father many times to let him go and join the war. The answer was always no. Darrell had often thought about running away to join the army, except he had two problems. The first problem was that the army was always fighting in Virginia, and that was too far to walk. The second problem was that even if he wanted to walk to Virginia, it would be hard to figure out where the army was. The only indication of the location of the Union troops came in stories in the *Dubaville Times* about the battles that they fought. But the newspaper stories appeared after the battles had taken place, and the army had probably moved on after the fighting. There simply was no way to determine the army's current position.

Now, thanks to the latest *Dubaville Times* news article, he knew exactly where the two armies were going, and he knew that they were within walking distance in Pennsylvania. It was a perfect coincidence! It was almost as if he was meant to run away, join the army, and come home a war hero! Darrell was never so excited about anything in his life. He could see it all clearly in his mind.

He saw himself fighting the rebels. He was saving Pennsylvania from the Confederate army. With each shot he takes, another soldier goes down. Finally, Robert E. Lee retreats and goes back to Virginia, shaking his fist in anger at Darrell. The *Dubaville Times* prints a story with the headline, "Darrell Stouffer Helps to Save Pennsylvania!" There is a big parade in his honor. The ladies of town line Main Street, waving handkerchiefs as Darrell passes. The children wave small American flags. His father is in the crowd, bragging to everyone that the boy parading down the street is his son. At the end of the street is a tall man with a beard. It is President Abraham Lincoln. He has a big medal, and attached to it is a red, white, and blue ribbon. When Darrell approaches, the president shakes his hand and gives him the medal.

It all seemed so real that it must be going to happen—Darrell knew it!

He decided that it was time to run away and join the army. He wasn't scared (well, maybe a little scared). He thought for a minute about how he was going to get away and then he thought of Kenny. This was perfect! Every time he had one of these great ideas, he always included Kenny. This one would be no exception. They were a team. What one did, the other was sure to follow. Why not get him to run away and join the army with him? Kenny would help him to settle down, and he would give him someone to talk to on the way to find the Union army.

"Hey, Mom!" Darrell yelled into the house from the front porch.

"Yes? What do you want?" I'm trying to get supper started," Mrs. Stouffer answered as she came to the front door.

"Can I go over to Kenny's house?" Darrell asked.

"Oh, I dunno about that. Your father is expecting you back in the woods. This was supposed to be a break, not the end of the day."

"But, Mom," Darrell complained, "I never get to see Kenny anymore. I couldn't go there yesterday because he had company. They left this morning. It's so hot today. Can't I go over there for just a little while? I promise I'll be home for supper."

"Your father's gonna be mad at me," Mrs. Stouffer said. Then she took a minute to think. "All right, but tomorrow you had better put in a full day's work!"

"I will, Mom. See you later."

Darrell ran to the McElroy farm. He found Kenny in the cornfield. The McElroy field was as large as the Stouffer's field, with row after row of corn plants. The stalks had only grown a little bit past Kenny's waist, and so it was easy for Darrell to locate him. Darrell ran up to him with the copy of the *Dubaville Times*.

"Hey, Kenny! Look what it says in the newspaper!"

Kenny could read, but it would take him a half an hour to get through the newspaper article, and even then he probably wouldn't get much out of it. He would rather have Darrell just tell him what the article was all about.

"What's in there that's got you so excited?" Kenny asked.

"It says here that the Confederate army is heading to Harrisburg."

"So what?"

"So if the rebs are heading to Harrisburg, the Union army has to be going to the same place," Darrell said to his best friend.

"Again, so what?" It was obvious that Kenny didn't share Darrell's enthusiasm.

"Don't you see? If the Union army is this near to us, we can go and join them."

"Darrell, how many times in the last two years have you asked your father if you could join the army? What makes you think he's gonna let you join now?"

"Who says I'm gonna ask him? I say we run away tonight and head toward Harrisburg. Most likely we'll run into our boys before we even make it there."

"Are you crazy? Why would I wanna run away to join the army?"

"Kenny, if we can whoop ole Bobby Lee and knock 'em back to Virginia, then we'll be war heroes! Everyone'll give us medals and parades. We'll be the youngest war heroes ever." Darrell wanted to grab Kenny and shake him to get him to do what he wanted him to do.

"First of all, there ain't a Union general who has beat Bobby Lee," Kenny said, standing his ground against Darrell's attacks. "He keeps outsmarting anybody ole Abe Lincoln has thrown at him. Second of all, if we run away from home, the only thing getting whooped will be my backside. I'm still smarting from our last prank with the snakes," Kenny said, rubbing his rear end.

"C'mon, Kenny. Don't you wanna be a part of history? No one will whoop us if we come back war heroes. Why, the whole town will honor us. How's your dad gonna punish us if we're heroes? He'd be the first one out there pinning medals on you."

"Yeah, and what happens if we come back looking like Terry McIntyre? You saw him when he first came back, all sad 'cuz he couldn't do nothing. What kind of a farmer am I gonna be with one leg?"

"We ain't gonna come back with one leg. We're faster than Terry ever was. And we're better shots than he is. There's no way them rebs are gonna hit us. We'll get them before they get us. C'mon, Kenny, we can do this!" Darrell pleaded.

"Why do you need me? Why don't you just go off and join the army by yourself? I don't really wanna get involved in this war. You're the one that's always talking about fighting in it."

Darrell was losing the battle. Never had Kenny stood up to him before. Every time he had an idea for some kind of caper, Kenny had always joined him—no questions asked. This wasn't a prank to pull on Mrs. Garber, but he still thought that Kenny should come with him. He could go by himself, but he always did things with Kenny. He really wanted Kenny to go with him.

If truth be known, he was a little scared of the stories that Terry McIntyre had told. One day Terry had taken off his bandage, and Darrell saw the scars on what was left of his leg. It was pretty frightening. The meaty part of his thigh just suddenly ended. The flesh had lines of scars where doctors had sewn skin to protect the wound.

Having Kenny with him would help calm him down some. But how could he get Kenny to change his mind? There was no way he could tell him that he was scared of what might lay ahead in battle. He had one last card to play that might change Kenny's mind.

"You're right, Kenny. I could go on my own. I could come back a war hero all by myself. People would ask me, 'How come Kenny wasn't with you? You two do everything together.' I'd have to tell them that Kenny was afraid to go and told me to go by myself. I could do that. I was just thinking that you would wanna go with me. We go everywhere together. But if you wanna break up our friendship because you're afraid of them rebels, then I guess I'll have to go by myself."

"I ain't afraid of nothing," Kenny said. "I ain't not going because I'm afraid. I ain't going because I don't wanna go."

"You keep telling yourself that, Kenny. But I know the real reason."

Darrell knew where to hit Kenny the hardest—his manhood. Kenny was the biggest, roughest boy in school. He always stood up to any challenge. Now Darrell was attacking the fact that Kenny wasn't afraid of anything.

"All right, I'll go," Kenny said. "But if I come back crippled, you'll have to live with that on your conscience. I don't care about this war—I care about this cornfield. But if you want me to go with you, then I'll do it. But this is it, Darrell. I'm tired of following you around and getting into trouble."

"We won't get into trouble—trust me. The Union army's gonna whip them rebs and send them outta Pennsylvania. They're in our land now. Our boys will fight harder to protect Pennsylvania. Even the new leader of the army is from Pennsylvania. The soldiers probably don't care about fighting in Virginia. We're gonna come back heroes. I promise. Now, wait till everyone's asleep. Then sneak out of your house, and I'll meet you in the meadow between our houses."

"What're we gonna eat? Harrisburg's a long ways away."

"Grab some food tonight before you go to bed. Bring your hunting rifle, and we can shoot something to eat along the way."

"You better watch yourself around Jeremiah tonight. You wake him, and you're in big trouble!"

"You worry about getting yourself down to the big meadow, and I'll worry about getting past Jeremiah. Now don't go falling asleep and forget about me!"

"Don't worry. I'll be there," Kenny said.

With that, the plan was made. Darrell had finally gotten what he wanted—a chance to go off and join the army. He was sure that he'd come back a war hero. He couldn't wait to gain honors for himself. He had missed being in the parade when the Dubaville boys went off to Harrisburg to enlist in 1861. After he helped to defeat the rebels trying to capture Harrisburg, he would have his own parade, and his parade would be even better than that first one.

He couldn't wait to get started.

# Chapter 6

# The Runaway from Home

It was the middle of the night when Darrell got up from his bed to sneak out of his house. His bedroom was dark, but light from the moon shining in the window helped Darrell to get past his sleeping brothers. The slightest noise might have woken Jeremiah, and he would have alerted his parents to the great escape attempt.

Before leaving the house, Darrell went into the kitchen. There he found some biscuits that he could eat on his journey. He then went to the barn where he had hidden a larger stash of food earlier in the day.

Darrell had been dreaming of this moment for a long time. He made his way from his house toward the big meadow where he was supposed to meet Kenny. He found a tree, sat down with his back against it, and waited for Kenny to arrive.

As he looked up at the clear, starry night, he knew that he faced two problems in bringing Kenny along. The first was keeping him fed. He had brought some food from home, but with Kenny's gigantic appetite that food wouldn't last very long. He had his hunting rifle to help to get more food, and he hoped that would be good enough. His second problem was occupying Kenny's time. Kenny got bored easily. He would have to think of things to do along the way or Kenny would lose interest. A bored and hungry Kenny would probably beg to turn around and go home.

Suddenly he heard loud noises coming through the brush. It had to be Kenny lumbering through the woods to join him. Kenny tripped and stumbled his way through life as he walked around. A couple of swear words came from the woods, indicating that Kenny must have run into something. Finally he emerged from the woods carrying a big sack of food. Darrell had to laugh at the size of the bag Kenny had brought to help feed himself.

"Where'd you get all that food?" Darrell asked amusedly.

"I just took some of what was lying around after dinner," Kenny answered, a little upset that Darrell was laughing at him.

"Man, that was lying around *after* dinner? That's more than what my mom sets out *for* dinner," Darrell responded, still playing around.

"Are we gonna get going, or are we gonna sit here all night making fun of my sack of food?" Kenny protested.

The two boys headed down the meadow to the road. They decided that they would walk two or three miles before stopping to sleep.

When they had walked that far, they went into the woods, built a fire to keep the mosquitoes away, and lay down to get a few hours of sleep.

In the morning, Darrell awoke to the sound of crunching. Kenny had awakened first and was tearing into his food sack for breakfast. He had already eaten almost half of the contents of his sack.

"Kenny, you better slow down. That food's gotta last you through the whole trip. You're going through it like there's no tomorrow."

"My mom says that breakfast is the most important meal of the day. She says that it's important to eat a big breakfast," Kenny mumbled through bites of a biscuit, trying to justify why he had eaten so much.

"You guys eat big breakfasts, big lunches, and big dinners. How can one be more important than the next?" Darrell playfully asked.

"My mom says that a hearty appetite is a sign of a healthy person," Kenny responded.

"Then you all are the healthiest people I know," Darrell said. He took out a little food to eat. He knew that he was going to have to save his food to give to Kenny when he ran out.

"Listen, Kenny. When we are walking today, we've got to keep watching for anyone coming down the road ahead of us or behind us. If we see anyone, we got to run back into the woods. We can't let anyone see us, or they'll run back home and tell our parents where we are. Got it?"

"*Mmmfffff!*" Kenny tried to say that he understood with his mouth full of food.

"Kenny, that's gotta be it for breakfast. I don't care how important the meal is—you gotta save something for later!"

"*Mmmfffff,*" Kenny repeated as he closed up his food sack.

Kenny and Darrell started off down the road, walking to Harrisburg. They had traveled maybe two miles when Kenny started getting bored.

"How far do you think we walked?" he asked his friend.

"Kenny, we've hardly walked five miles between last night and today. It's almost sixty to Harrisburg. We've got a long way to go. That's why I told you to take it easy on eating your food. It's gonna take us a long time to meet up with the Union army."

They walked in silence for a while, and then Kenny turned back to Darrell.

"You think we've walked a mile since the last time I asked you?"

"Kenny, if you keep asking how far we've gotten every ten minutes, you'll drive me crazy before we get to Harrisburg."

"I was just asking, that's all," Kenny responded.

Darrell knew he was in trouble. He had to occupy Kenny's mind with something to take it off the length of the walk. And then a brilliant idea came to him.

"Hey, Kenny. As we walk, let's think up some games to play against each other. We can keep track of how many each one of us wins, and then we'll crown the 'King of the Walk' when we're done walking."

"That's a great idea. What do we do first?" Kenny asked, all excited.

Darrell had to think of something that Kenny could win. If he could keep Kenny ahead in the competition for a while, he could keep Kenny busy thinking up new games. Kenny was big, and farming had made him strong, so he came up with a competition that would take advantage of his physique.

"Let's play Flinch," Darrell invented. "You hit me in the arm as hard as you can, and then I hit you. We keep on punching each other until one of us flinches or cries 'uncle.' You go first!"

Kenny smiled and reared back and walloped Darrell in the upper section of his right arm. The force stung Darrell and sent a tingling feeling down his arm. The blow was much stronger than he had anticipated. He tried to duplicate its force when he hit Kenny, but it clearly had no effect on him, as Kenny giggled after the punch.

"Is that all you got? My sister hits harder than that," he taunted Darrell. Then he struck Darrell in the exact same spot of his first punch with even greater force, and a black-and-blue mark grew instantly on Darrell's arm. Darrell's second blow had less of an effect than the first one seeing he was right-handed and Kenny's punches had taken a lot of the power from his blows. Kenny smiled, and he moved in for the kill. Darrell clearly had had enough, and cried uncle before Kenny's third punch was thrown.

"I win! I'm ahead of you one game to zero!" Kenny yelled exultantly. Kenny was always second to Darrell in everything they did, and he smiled at the thought that he was actually ahead of Darrell at something. Kenny's mind was occupied with trying to come up with new games where he could beat Darrell.

The two boys walked a few more miles. The sun was hot, but they walked in the shade of the trees growing along one side of the dirt road. The path twisted and turned, and then the boys came to a long stretch of straight road.

"Hey, I got an idea for a game," Darrell said. "Let's have a running race. We'll start here, and the first one to reach that old oak tree lying near the road way up there wins the race."

"I dunno," Kenny said.

"Come on, Kenny. I'll even let you call the start of the race."

"Okay. Get on your mark . . . get set, go!" Kenny yelled, trying to sneak a head start by speeding up the call for the start of the race.

Darrell didn't really care. He could've given Kenny a large head start and still beat him. Kenny's size made for punching power, but it was a drawback in running. Darrell sped past Kenny and easily won the race. They each had one victory apiece.

Darrell's plan was working. Kenny wasn't complaining about how long they'd been walking; he was too busy thinking about games to play. They walked another couple of miles and then came upon a large cluster of apple trees. This was Kenny's area of strength: eating! Darrell wanted to keep Kenny in the lead of the competition for a while, and the apple trees provided him with a way to do it.

"Kenny, let's have an eating race. We each get five apples. The first one who eats them all up wins."

"Now this is something I'm good at. I might not be a fast runner, but I sure am a fast eater," Kenny said, delighted with the new challenge.

The competition was about as close as Darrell's running race. Darrell had just started eating his third apple when Kenny had finished his fifth and was digging into the two apples that Darrell hadn't touched yet. By the time Darrell had finished that third apple, Kenny had polished off his other two. Kenny was delighted in his victory. He was up two games to one. The two rested for a few minutes, and then Kenny picked another ten or twelve apples to eat along the way.

The boys continued walking down the dirt road. They started to become really thirsty between the heat of the day and the dust that they were kicking up by walking. Kenny spotted a pond near the road, and the boys hurried over to it to get a drink.

"Hey, Kenny," Darrell said, after he had thought up a new game. "You wanna skip stones? The one who can make a rock skip the most times wins."

The boys looked for smooth, flat stones. Kenny got to throw first. He felt the pressure to set the pace with a good throw. But he threw his stone at the wrong angle, and he was lucky to get three skips before his rock plunked into the water.

"That's all you got? My little sister can skip a rock better than that," Darrell taunted Kenny with the words Kenny had used earlier. Then Darrell whipped off a throw where his stone skipped nine times before eventually falling into the water. Kenny was in big trouble. He had to have a good second throw, but he could only coax six skips from his second rock. Darrell figured his first throw would be the winner, and barely got five skips from his half-hearted second throw. Kenny again felt the pressure, and his third throw plopped straight down into the water without a single skip as Darrell laughed.

"Nice throw, Kenny. Where was the skip?"

"That ain't funny. The rock slipped outta my hand," Kenny lied. "I should get another chance."

"Even Jeremiah can get a rock to skip once," Darrell laughed. "We're tied at two games each. Let's look for something to do for another game."

The competition had focused both boys' attention so much that walking became fun. They laughed and joked together as they walked along the dusty road. Enjoying their friendship was the most important thing at the moment. The two boys came upon a crab apple tree. The fruit was about as big as a cherry.

"We can use these crab apples like ammunition," Darrell said. "We'll play soldier. The first one that hits the enemy wins."

Each boy grabbed a shirt-full amount of ammo. They hid behind trees firing at each other. The safety of their hiding places made it hard to kill the enemy. Darrell decided to move out into the open to get a better shot at his friend. He ran at Kenny, hit the ground real fast, rolled through the dirt, and came up firing at his enemy, but Kenny had secured himself behind a big oak tree, and the crab apples whizzed past him.

"I thought you were a good shot. You ain't even coming close to me," Kenny bragged.

Then Darrell crawled on his belly to get closer and aimed at the right side of the tree. When Kenny would think it was safe to come out firing, Darrell's crab apple would be on its way first. But if Kenny came out on the left side of the tree, Darrell would be in a vulnerable position and would be a sitting duck for Kenny's shot. Darrell guessed right, and as Kenny peeked around the right side of the tree, Darrell's shot hit him right in the forehead.

"Oooh, you got me!" Kenny pretended to moan. Then he staggered around in circles, and he overacted a stumbling movement until he fell dead in the middle of the road, lying spread eagle. They both laughed, and Darrell reminded Kenny that he was in the lead three games to two.

"I'm gonna be a great soldier," Darrell bragged to Kenny. "See how easy it is for me to hit the enemy."

"I saw you lying in the road. If there was more than one of me coming from behind the tree, you'd be dead."

"You're just sore that I shot you," Darrell protested. "If there were two of you, I'd of got both of you. I've been waiting for almost three years to get into this war. I tell you, I'm gonna win all kinds of medals for bravery. Just ole Bobby Lee wait till I get into the fighting. He'll wish he never came to Pennsylvania."

"Yeah, but nobody beats Bobby Lee, Darrell. What if we're walking to another disaster of the Union army?"

"We're gonna win—just you wait and see," Darrell confidently spoke.

They continued walking, and Kenny found two big rocks halfway buried in the ground. His game was to dig up a rock and then lift it over your head. The rocks weighed about fifty pounds each. Both boys started clawing at the dirt to try to free their boulders. Darrell started kicking the top of his rock to loosen it, but he hadn't dug out very much dirt, and so the rock never budged an inch. Kenny uncovered more dirt, pushed his boulder until it rolled out of its hole, and triumphantly elevated it over his head. The competition was tied again at three games apiece.

The sun was high in the sky. Darrell's competition had worked wonders in occupying Kenny's time and keeping his thoughts off food. But Kenny's stomach ran on an internal clock, and it knew when it was lunchtime and it was supposed to get fed again. No game could take the place of eating.

"I'm hungry. Let's stop and eat lunch," Kenny pleaded.

"Hey, I know a good game. Let's hunt for our lunch. The first person to shoot a rabbit or a pheasant wins," Darrell proposed. He wanted to keep Kenny away from his food sack for as long as possible. The boys split up and made their way into the woods.

After a few minutes, Darrell came upon a big ring-necked pheasant. He inched closer to the bird, aimed, and fired.

The two boys now had something delicious to eat for lunch. Kenny came running over when he heard the shot.

"Look at this beauty," Darrell showed Kenny. "I shoot it—you cook it. Those are the rules! The winner never cleans the kill."

Darrell gloated, but Kenny had the feathers off and the bird cooking on a fire in no time. The two friends sat back and ate their fill. Even though Kenny ate two thirds of the bird, Darrell was satisfied with what he had to eat. Kenny had sneaked into his food sack while the pheasant was cooking, but Darrell convinced him to save some for later instead of finishing off both the food supply and the bird that he had killed.

After lunch, the boys decided that they earned a long break. They both lay back and took a nap. The boys slept about a half an hour before getting up and resuming their walk. Once again, Darrell woke up to find Kenny in his food sack. He couldn't help but think that Kenny was too obsessed with food. He had to convince him once more to conserve his food supply.

The boys continued on the road to Harrisburg. Kenny walked in silence for a while and then turned to Darrell.

"Hey, Darrell. Why do you like this war so much?"

"It's not that I like the war; I believe in what we're fighting for. No state has the right to just up and quit on the United States."

"My dad says that we ain't fighting for bringing back the Southern states no more. He says we're fighting to free the slaves. My dad says that's why Mr. Lincoln has so much trouble getting people to sign up to fight. They don't want to free the slaves."

"Why don't people want to free the slaves, Kenny?"

"My dad says that people are afraid that when the blacks are freed they'll all come up north and take away all the good jobs."

"But your dad's a farmer, Kenny. Why does he have to be afraid of the blacks coming north and taking jobs?"

"My dad says that some blacks will come up here and start growing corn. If they grow corn and we grow corn, then when we take our crop to the market, we won't get as much money cuz there are too many people out there growing corn."

"That's crazy! Do you think that there are all of these slaves sitting down South thinking that they can't wait for the Union army to win so that they can come up to Pennsylvania and grow corn?" Darrell teased.

"You don't know, Darrell. You don't know what them black people will do if they're freed."

Darrell didn't want to get Kenny mad. He knew Kenny got most of his views of life from his parents. He wanted Kenny to think for himself about the war and slavery.

"I may not know what the slaves would do if they were freed, Kenny, but I do know that the white people down South treat their slaves bad. They beat on those people. They sell their moms and dads away from their children. How'd you feel if your dad was sold away from your house one day?"

"I don't think I'd like it much. They can have my sister Kate, though. She's gettin' to be a big pain."

"Yeah, and I'd love to sell 'em Jeremiah. Maybe we could sell them both together!" Darrell laughed with Kenny. "Seriously though. Maybe ole Abe ain't so wrong about wanting to free the slaves after all. I read that book that Mrs. Garber has—*Uncle Tom's Cabin*. Kenny, they beat that man—Uncle Tom. They beat that man till he was dead. Shouldn't no man be treated like that—I don't care what color his skin is. Yeah, I think Mr. Lincoln did a good thing passing that law that gives slaves their freedom—you know, that emancipation thing that Mrs. Garber told us about in school. Now we just gotta win this war to make it stick."

"But nobody can beat General Lee. He always wins," Kenny uttered.

"I keep telling you: he ain't never been to Pennsylvania before. Wait till good ole Pennsylvania boys get a hold of his army. They'll make him wish he stayed in Virginia. And we'll be there to be a part of it. Aren't you excited about that, Kenny?"

"I guess so. I just don't like this war like you do. We better come home heroes, or I'm not gonna be able to sit down for a week!"

The two boys walked for a little while in silence, and then Darrell turned to Kenny.

"Kenny, why do you like farming so much?"

"I dunno. It's the only thing I'm really good at. I don't know much about too many things, but I know farming. I like that."

"But what is it about farming that you like so much?" Darrell persisted.

"I like planting in the spring. I like watching over the fields every day after the planting. Each plant is like a little kid. You gotta take care of 'em all the time. You worry that they don't have enough water. Then you worry that they're getting too much of it. The best time is when the corn stalks grow so tall that I can go in the middle of the field, lay down in it, and hide away from everyone. I just lay there and think."

Darrell was impressed that Kenny could express himself so well when it came to farming. It was obvious that Kenny liked it much more than Darrell did.

"What do you think about out there in the cornfield, Kenny?"

"I think about a lot of stuff. I think of you and me farming next to each other all our lives. We'll have big families and our kids will play together like we did."

Darrell laughed and said, "You think you'll be marrying Maggie? Your kids will turn out looking like carrots with all that red, frizzy hair on top."

"Who says I'm marrying Maggie Kirkpatrick? Just cuz I walked her home after school that one day—and that was because of you, Darrell Stouffer. If you didn't have to bring snakes into school, I wouldn't have had to walk her home."

"I heard you held her hand all the way," Darrell lied.

"I didn't touch that ugly thing. She's probably got all kinds of bugs on her just waiting to jump off onto the first person who comes near her."

"You say that now, Kenny. You just wait. I bet in a year or two you'll change your mind, and you'll be looking at her all lovey-dovey."

"Take that back, Darrell Stouffer. And what about you? Who are you gonna get lovey-dovey over?" Kenny complained.

"I don't like any girl—and no girl has their eyes on me either. I like it that way," Darrell answered. Then he thought for a moment. "I dunno, Kenny. I don't like farming like you do. I don't know why. I guess it's like me and you with soldiering. You don't like that as much as I do."

"But you gotta like farming, Darrell. One day you'll take over your dad's farm. Then we'll farm together."

Darrell thought about taking over his father's farm. He'd have to work through all of the hot summers. He'd have to make sure the crop was harvested in time. He'd have to get the corn to the market to make money to be able to plant the next year's crop. He began to doubt if that was what he really wanted to do.

"I used to think that I was meant to do something other than farming," he said to Kenny. "What it was, I don't know. I thought that going to school would help show me the path I was supposed to take in life, but we both know that schooling's over, and I never figured out what I was supposed to do. I feel kinda stuck at being a farmer. I thought if you told me why you liked it, maybe I could learn to like it more, too."

"Go lay down among the corn stalks. You can't dislike farming after doing that," Kenny suggested. "I think that every year growing corn is like seeing God's little miracles springing up from the ground. It starts out with these little seeds, and after a few months, you got this field full of corn. Sit out there and watch the miracle happen."

"I guess," Darrell sighed, still uncertain of his future. The two boys walked for a while in silence.

All of a sudden Kenny had an idea. That was a pretty rare thing for him. He usually let Darrell come up with the things that they would do.

"Hey, Darrell," he said excitedly. "I got a good idea."

"Yeah, Kenny, what's that?"

"Instead of turning north at the next road to Harrisburg, if we stay on the road that we're on, we'll end up at my aunt and uncle's house. We can get a good dinner, sleep in a nice, comfortable bed, and then head back out on the road tomorrow morning."

"I dunno. Don't you think it's risky staying with family? Don't you think that they'll want us to go back home instead of going off to war?"

"Nah, my aunt and uncle aren't like that. They'll let us go to Harrisburg in the morning. My uncle fought in the Mexican War. He knows what soldiering's like. C'mon Darrell. I'm gonna be real hungry at suppertime, and my Aunt Clara is a real fine cook. Let's go eat dinner there."

"All right. I guess if we stayed out on the road tonight, I'd have to kill a bear for you to eat, and you'd still be sneaking into your food sack. By the way, Kenny, where do your aunt and uncle live?"

Kenny said, "They live in Gettysburg."

# Chapter 7

# THE ARRIVAL IN GETTYSBURG

It was late afternoon when Kenny and Darrell came to the crest of a hill. Below them was the town of Gettysburg. They could see that there were a few white-painted houses leading into the town. A white, wooden fence ran alongside the road that they were traveling on. When the boys came into Gettysburg, the houses were closer together. Many had red brick exteriors.

The boys were dirty from the long walk; they were walking barefoot, and they were carrying their hunting rifles. They figured that their disheveled look was making Gettysburg residents nervous, because when the townspeople saw them, they gave the boys strange looks and ran away.

"I don't get it," Kenny said. "The people in Gettysburg are usually the nicest kind of folks. They've always been great when we came to visit my aunt and uncle."

"They ain't so nice today, though," Darrell answered.

"I dunno," Kenny said. "But I'm not sure how to get to Carlisle Street from here. That's where my uncle lives. We gotta find someone to give us directions."

They walked a couple of blocks and saw an old woman sitting in a rocking chair on her front porch. She looked like a kindly woman. Kenny decided to ask her for directions.

"Excuse me, ma'am. Can you help us? We're looking for Carlisle Street," Kenny asked as politely as he could.

The old lady scowled at the boys and stood up quickly. As she made a move to her front door, she angrily sneered, "I ain't gonna help you one bit. Why don't you go back to where you came from?" With that, she stormed into her house and slammed the door behind her.

"I see what you were talking about, Kenny. These are the nicest people I ever met," Darrell chuckled with sarcasm.

"I don't get it," Kenny said again, shaking his head. "I love coming to Gettysburg cuz the people make you feel welcome. Today they're treating us like we've got a disease or something."

"Let's just keep walking, and maybe we can find someone who'll help us," Darrell suggested.

The boys continued walking down the street, getting more strange looks from the residents as they continued to look for Carlisle Street. While walking down one of the main roads of town, they stumbled across the street sign for the road that they were looking for. The third house down Carlisle Street was the McElroy residence. As the boys turned up the path to the house, Kenny saw his Aunt Clara in the backyard taking down her laundry from the clothesline. They headed to the rear of the house to say hello.

"Hi, Aunt Clara!" Kenny yelled from a few feet away.

"Oh my goodness! Kenneth John McElroy, come here and give your aunt a big hug!" Aunt Clara McElroy shouted with joy at seeing her nephew. Kenny went over to her and put his arms around his aunt, but he didn't want to get real close because his clothes were all dirty. He didn't have a choice, as Aunt Clara grasped him tightly. As they ended their embrace, Kenny turned to introduce Darrell.

"Aunt Clara, this is my best friend, Darrell Stouffer."

"Hi, Mrs. McElroy. It's a pleasure to meet you," Darrell said holding out his hand to shake Aunt Clara's. Aunt Clara shook Darrell's hand, and then looked perplexed over the boys' shoulders.

"Kenny, where's your mother and father? How come you didn't let us know that you were coming for a visit?"

Kenny was at a loss for words. He kicked the ground a little and couldn't look his aunt straight in the eyes. He knew this question was going to come, but he never came up with a good answer to it, other than the truth.

"Uh—um, my parents aren't with us. We—uh—sorta ran away from home to—um—join the army. Our parents don't know that we're here." Kenny turned red in embarrassment. He waited for his aunt to start yelling at him.

Darrell interrupted to try to save his friend. "We just wanna be there to kick ole General Lee out of Pennsylvania. Then we plan to go back home right away."

"You two boys ran away? I don't think I like that. And to join the army? Kenny, we can't just let you go from here to get involved in the war. What if something should happen to you? Your dad would never forgive us for not stopping you. When your Uncle Levi gets home from the store tonight, we'll have to talk this over."

"Yes, ma'am," Kenny mumbled, upset with himself for having suggested that they come to Gettysburg in the first place. Aunt Clara saw the troubled look on Kenny's face.

"Don't worry, Kenny. We'll think of something when your Uncle Levi gets home. In the meantime, why don't you boys wash up. You look like something that the cat dragged in. Elizabeth, come outside and say hi to your cousin and his friend!" Aunt Clara bellowed.

Out of the back door came Kenny's cousin, Elizabeth McElroy. She was about the same age as Darrell and Kenny. She had long blonde hair that was tied into a braid, and she was wearing a lavender-colored dress. When Darrell saw Elizabeth, he didn't know what to do. Kenny had never told him that he had such a pretty cousin in Gettysburg. His heart beat faster than it had ever done before. He couldn't even get his mouth to work to say hello, and so he kept silent.

"Hi, Elizabeth," Kenny said dejectedly. He and Elizabeth didn't get along too well. He would have preferred to have a male cousin so he could have someone to do things with. Elizabeth always wanted to do girly things like playing with dolls. Kenny didn't have much to do with her. "This here's my friend, Darrell Stouffer."

"Hi, Darrell," Elizabeth said in a voice that almost sounded like singing. Darrell just stood there looking at her, dumbfounded. This feeling was new to him. No girl in Dubaville had ever made him look so stupid. He also knew that he had better find a way to hide his feelings, because if Kenny caught wind of the fact that he was fond of his cousin, there would be no end to his teasing.

"Elizabeth, fetch some water so these boys can wash up. You boys hungry? You want a snack to tide you over until supper?" Aunt Clara suggested, being the graceful host.

"Yeah!" Kenny said, suddenly springing back to life at the sound of food.

"Elizabeth, set out some of those cookies that we baked today. These boys have walked a far piece and need something to eat," Aunt Clara ordered.

"Kenny, where's Uncle William and Aunt Sarah?" Elizabeth asked.

"Never you mind that," Aunt Clara butted in to save Kenny from another awkward moment. "You just run along and do what I asked you to do."

The boys felt better after washing up. Darrell let Kenny have all of the cookies that Elizabeth set out for them. He felt bad that Kenny was put in a tough situation. He knew suppertime wouldn't be easy, either. Kenny's Uncle Levi was bound to come down hard on Kenny—Levi being his father's younger brother.

Uncle Levi McElroy owned a general store in Gettysburg. He ran the business by himself. He worked long hours, getting to the store before many residents were awake, and staying to count inventory until well after eight o'clock in the evening. When he finally came home, dinner was always on the table—something Clara McElroy took great pride in.

That evening, Aunt Clara stopped Uncle Levi as he came into the house to tell him that they had visitors. Darrell and Kenny squirmed a little, afraid of how everything was going to work out.

Levi McElroy was a calm man and didn't get too upset over troubles. Before saying anything that night, he had to decide on the best action to take. He knew he had to protect his brother's family. Letting Kenny run off and join the Union army was simply out of the question. But how he would approach Kenny on the subject would take some tact.

Everyone took a seat around the table. Kenny was so nervous that for the first time in his life he didn't dig right into his supper. He pushed the food around a little with his fork. Uncle Levi looked at the boys.

"Your Aunt Clara tells me you boys ran away from home to join the army. Is that right?"

"Yes sir," Kenny mumbled.

"You think the army needs a couple of thirteen-year-old boys? If it does, maybe we're in bigger trouble than I thought," Uncle Levi said, sounding more like their fathers instead of Kenny's uncle.

Kenny just sat there, unable to say anything. Darrell looked at his friend, and then he began to explain the reasons why they had run away from home.

"We wanna help the army beat General Lee. We heard that everyone was heading for Harrisburg. It was in our newspaper. We figured that we could meet up with the army and help them win the battle. They're in our state. Why shouldn't we help kick the rebs out?" Darrell reasoned.

"You boys know what you're gettin' into? I fought in a war before—down in Mexico. It's not all glamour and glory. War is a lot of suffering and dying. So if you two were going to Harrisburg, how come you ended up in Gettysburg? Aren't we a little out of your way?"

Darrell grew excited talking about going to war. "On our way to Harrisburg, Kenny remembered that you lived close by. He told me that we couldn't go any further without stopping here and seeing everyone. He said that I had to meet his Aunt Clara, and that she was the best cook of anyone around. We decided that since we were in the area, that we should stop and pay you a visit." Darrell was trying to help Kenny by making him seem more dedicated to his family. Uncle Levi saw through his plan, and smiled to himself.

"I don't think you have to go all the way to Harrisburg to find the rebel army, do you Levi?" Aunt Clara interrupted.

"She's right. Why, Southern soldiers have been in and out of Gettysburg for the last few days. Every time they show up, they stir up the citizens," Uncle Levi explained.

"Your Uncle Levi thinks that they're coming to town in search of shoes, isn't that right Levi?" Aunt Clara laughed.

"A lot of them rebs walked barefoot all the way up here from Virginia. I bet they heard we got a few places in town that make shoes. They came here the other day demanding all sorts of supplies. I bet the next time they come to town, they'll be after shoes," Uncle Levi bitterly remarked.

"Wait!" exclaimed Darrell. "You say that the rebs came to town barefoot and stirred up all the people?"

"That's right," Uncle Levi answered.

"Kenny, I bet that's why everyone was acting so funny earlier. I bet they saw us as strangers in bare feet with rifles, and figured we was Southern soldiers. Hey, that's pretty funny," Darrell said.

"Yea, I'll betcha that's what happened," Uncle Levi responded. "People have been on edge for a few days now. They're especially nervous around strangers. Dave Redunski said that he saw a unit of Union cavalry dig in north of town. He says the people up there are mighty happy to see some of our boys for a change."

"Really!" Darrell said, getting all excited. "Some of our soldiers are that close by. Think we can go see 'em in the morning—not to join up, but just to see 'em?"

"I don't know. Redunski thinks that it's good having the soldiers up there. I told him that it might be a bad thing," Uncle Levi said.

"Why's that, Levi?" Aunt Clara asked.

"Well, if Lee's army is looking for someone to fight, there they are. They could be bringing the whole blooming Confederate army right to our doorstep," Uncle Levi said.

"That's ridiculous," Aunt Clara said. She was trying to keep Elizabeth from getting upset.

"Well, I guess it's a good thing you boys did come to town. With me at the store, it'll be good to have you two around to help the womenfolk. If there is any action, I'll need you two to watch over 'em," Uncle Levi said.

"We'd be glad to do it, isn't that right, Darrell?" Kenny said. When he saw that he wasn't in as much trouble as he thought he'd be in, he started eating his supper. Everything was all was right with Kenny's world again.

"Now, Levi, if some of them Southerners come into town looking for supplies, you just give them anything they want. I don't need to become a widow just because you can't part with a little bit of food and stuff," Aunt Clara said to her husband.

"That stuff is what keeps us fed and clothed. If I go giving it away, we'll lose our business. I'm hiding everything I can before the rebs come back. They won't find nothing they need in my store," Uncle Levi said. "The last time a group of soldiers came into town, they cleaned out Daniel Porter's store. They gave him some Confederate money for what they took, but I hear that their money is just worthless paper."

After dinner, the boys were really tired and went upstairs to the guest bedroom to go to sleep.

"What do you think we should do tomorrow?" Kenny asked.

"Your uncle asked us to hang around, and so I think we ought to stay here—at least for one more day." What Darrell really wanted to do was be around Elizabeth more, but blaming Kenny's uncle allowed him to hide this fact.

"I'm sorry that I screwed things up, Darrell. I know you want to try to find the army, and we can't do it from here in Gettysburg."

"I don't know, Kenny. Maybe your uncle's right. Maybe that Union cavalry unit north of town will be like a beacon, signaling General Lee where to find the enemy. Maybe the Union army will come to Gettysburg to help the cavalry," Darrell hopefully contended.

Suddenly there was a light tap at the door. It was barely audible. The door silently opened, and Elizabeth sneaked into the room.

"What are you doing in here?" Kenny questioned angrily.

"Shhhh! Kenny, keep it down. If my father knew I was in here, I'd be in big trouble," Elizabeth whispered. "I didn't get a chance to talk to you two before. I just want to talk for a little while."

Darrell didn't have any problem with Elizabeth being in the room. She was clad in her pink bathrobe that stretched down to the floor. Plus, it was fun watching Kenny get upset when he had to deal with his cousin.

"Are you two really going to join the army?" Elizabeth asked.

"Yeah, and we're gonna fight them rebels, too," Kenny said.

"I read the newspapers all of the time. After every battle, they list the names of the dead and wounded. Lots of boys on each side are dying. Aren't you afraid of getting hurt?" Elizabeth asked, showing that she cared for the boys. Kenny looked at his cousin differently. Maybe for the first time in his life, he was talking with Elizabeth as if she were a real person.

"We're gonna be all right," Kenny said. "Darrell says that we're faster than the other soldiers. We won't get hit. Ain't that right, Darrell?"

"Yeah," Darrell said. "But we promised your father that we would hang close to the house tomorrow in case something happens. We aren't gonna run away to fight tomorrow—so you can relax, Elizabeth."

"I saw some of those rebel soldiers when they came to town. They look mean. I was real scared when they were here. They took lots of stuff from our neighbors. They left our house alone, though," Elizabeth nervously said. "You think that they'll attack tomorrow in Gettysburg like my dad said at dinner?"

"Nah, there's only a little cavalry unit north of town. Lee's looking for the infantry, not the cavalry," Darrell lied. He secretly hoped that there would be a battle—that way he could join the army right here in town.

"That's good," Elizabeth said, and she flashed her pretty smile. Her eyes lit up with the smile. As Darrell looked at her, part of him wanted to yell out his feelings for her, but he knew that would be a bad thing. His heart pounded so loudly that he thought it would beat right out of his body. What worried him was that he didn't know if Elizabeth liked him. That was the hardest thing about love—waiting until you were sure that the other person felt the same way about you before you let them know your feelings. That way you didn't look like a dope if you said that you liked someone and they told you that they didn't like you.

Elizabeth had slipped out of the room and gone back to her own bedroom.

How would Darrell find out if Elizabeth liked him? He wished for the good old days when he didn't care that much for girls. This love stuff was mighty perplexing! He was sure that Kenny was going to find out how much he liked his cousin. Then he would be harassed continuously. Darrell was forever making fun of Kenny because of Maggie Kirkpatrick. This would be Kenny's chance to get even with him.

It didn't take Kenny and Darrell much time before they were asleep. The day had been a long one, but the next few days were going to be a lot longer.

# Chapter 8

## THE FIRST SHOTS OF THE BATTLE

The first day of July started out like any other day for Uncle Levi McElroy. He was up before dawn. He grabbed something to eat, and he got ready to take off to his store. Darrell had also awakened early.

"I want you to stay close to the house today, Darrell," Uncle Levi said. "I don't know what's going to happen with the cavalry north of town, but it will help the women to settle down if you and Kenny are nearby."

"We'll hang around," Darrell reassured him.

"I need to be at my store in case some Confederate soldiers try to break in and take everything in it. If I can hide some of the items that they want, maybe I can save my store."

"Do you want Kenny to stay here and me to go and help you?" Darrell asked.

"Nah, I'll take care of the store, but thanks for asking," Uncle Levi said.

Uncle Levi liked Darrell. He had the boldness that Levi had when he was younger. When Uncle Levi wanted to join the army to fight in the Mexican War, his father was against it. Levi didn't care and went off to fight anyway. Looking at Darrell, he saw that same spunk. He was supposed to be angry with Darrell and Kenny for running away to join the Union army, but remembering his own youthful years, he had a difficult time coming down hard on them. The big difference, though, was that Darrell and Kenny were only thirteen years old. He had gone off to war at the age of nineteen.

The rest of the members of the house were awake and moving not long after the sun came up. When he saw that his Aunt Clara was cooking a big breakfast, Kenny smiled. If he and Darrell had decided to camp out somewhere on the road instead of staying with his aunt and uncle, he would probably be starving this morning. Here there was plenty of food. He ran to the breakfast table and began to eat heartily. Elizabeth and Darrell together couldn't match the amount of food Kenny was chowing down.

As the four gathered around the table, enjoying each other's company, there was also an air of nervousness, as they were wondering what was going to happen with the cavalry unit north of town. Uncle Levi had been certain that the unit would attract parts of the Southern army. Was the Union cavalry there for a reason? Did they know that Southern troops were close by? Were more Union troops near in case the cavalry got into a skirmish? Darrell thought about these questions as he was eating.

All of a sudden there were noises of gunfire and cannons bursting. The blasts startled the four residents of the McElroy house. Aunt Clara, Darrell, and Kenny ran out to the street to see what was going on. Elizabeth stayed inside. When the three got outdoors, they saw other residents already in the street. They went to where a cluster of people had gathered.

Everyone was looking up to the roof of the McElroy's next-door neighbor, the Johnsons. Little Johnny Johnson had fearlessly climbed up the side of the house and was on top of his roof. He was trying to see the battle.

"Can you see anything, son?" Mr. Johnson yelled up.

"All I see is a lot of smoke," little Johnny yelled back down.

"Smoke?" Darrell asked Mr. Johnson.

"He probably means the gun smoke from all of the rifles and cannons firing," Mr. Johnson answered. "Can you see any of the soldiers, Johnny?"

"I can see a few of them, but they're so far away," Johnny told his father.

Darrell was getting excited. This is what he ran away to see—the battle between Lee's army and the Union army. Actually he had wanted to take part in the battle, but he figured seeing it was the next best thing. He had promised Uncle Levi earlier that he wouldn't grab his gun if he heard the sounds of battle. He also had promised to stick around the house to help Aunt Clara and Elizabeth. But how could he miss out on going to the battle? He had to find a way to get north of town.

"A lot of us are gonna head up closer to the battle. You boys wanna join us?" Mr. Johnson asked Darrell and Kenny.

"I don't think I like that," Aunt Clara interrupted. "I don't want to see the boys get hurt."

"We'll stay as far away from the action as we can, Mrs. McElroy," Darrell pleaded. He had his opening to find a way to get to the battle, and he had to pursue it. "We promise we won't get anywhere near the real fighting."

"I'll keep an eye on them for you, Clara," Mr. Johnson replied. "They'll be all right with me."

"I don't know. I don't like sending boys so young so close to all that shooting," Aunt Clara said uneasily.

"We promise to be careful, Mrs. McElroy. Please, can we go with Mr. Johnson?" Darrell beseeched.

Kenny didn't say very much. He wasn't scared, but he also didn't want to get that close to the battle.

"Okay, you boys stay close to Mr. Johnson. When he says it's time to come home, you listen to him," Aunt Clara finally relented.

Darrell couldn't wait to see the fighting up close. Mr. Johnson left his son, little Johnny, up on his roof and followed a few other residents up the street toward the battle. Mr. Johnson was a nice man, but Darrell was about to learn two things about him that would delay their journey to the fighting. The first was that he knew everyone in town, and he felt the need to stop and talk to each and every person that he knew. The second thing was that he was a talker. He could talk for hours without saying very much. Mr. Johnson was a lawyer by trade, and he used his gift of gab to argue for his clients.

Mr. Johnson made it to the street corner before he found his first conversation. He stopped an old-timer whom he knew. He began a long speech about how this war was different from the one that the old-timer had previously fought in. Darrell anxiously kicked at the dirt, waiting for Mr. Johnson to stop talking. Then Mr. Johnson shook the old man's hand, and the group started off toward the battle again.

They had only walked half a block before Mr. Johnson greeted a woman. He told the lady that his son had climbed up on his roof to see the battle. He described for her what little Johnny had seen. Darrell looked impatiently at Kenny.

"We'll never get to the battlefield if he stops to talk to everybody in Gettysburg," he complained.

"We promised my Aunt Clara that we would stay with him, though," Kenny said. "We're not gonna go on without him. I'm not so sure that we're doing the right thing leaving my aunt and Elizabeth alone."

"Don't worry, Kenny. Everything'll work out. I promise, we'll never get that close to the action," Darrell said to his friend. "Look, I think Mr. Johnson's finally done talking to this lady. Maybe we can get him more than a few steps farther before he finds someone else to talk to."

Mr. Johnson made two more stops to talk as they headed northward. Darrell grew more and more impatient. He felt like he did when he had to accompany his mother to the general store back in Dubaville. She would always promise that she was only going to buy a couple of things, and then she would constantly stop and examine different items all over the store. Darrell would have to wait at the counter until his mother finally decided that she was done looking and ready to buy. He hated waiting for her to make up her mind just much as he hated waiting for Mr. Johnson to stop talking to people.

Mr. Johnson made his way down the next whole block before finding someone else to talk to. The sounds of battle were getting louder, and it seemed as if they were calling to Darrell. He finally had enough. Just as Mr. Johnson was getting into a good conversation about how hot the weather had been over the past few weeks, Darrell decided that he and Kenny were going to go on ahead. He did not bother to check with Kenny to see what he thought of his decision.

"Mr. Johnson. Kenny and I are gonna go ahead a little. We'll look for you when you get up closer to the battlefield."

Mr. Johnson didn't want to end his discussion, and he waved the boys on forward. Darrell took it as a sign to go, but Kenny was hesitant.

"We promised my aunt, Darrell," he said.

"We'll just go a little ahead, and we'll keep an eye out for Mr. Johnson. If we wait for him to stop talking, the whole war'll be over. It'll be okay, Kenny."

"But you said that we would stick with Mr. Johnson. Darrell, this isn't a prank that we're trying to pull on Mrs. Garber. This is serious. I don't think we should do something that we promised my aunt that we wouldn't do," Kenny said.

It was obvious to Darrell that Kenny was nervous about going closer to the fighting. He was going to have to work harder to convince him to leave Mr. Johnson.

"Look, Kenny," Darrell said. "We won't get anywhere close to the action. I just wanna see what's going on up there. Don't worry. Mr. Johnson'll be right behind us. Come on. It'll be all right."

Darrell didn't stop to wait for Kenny's response. He was walking fast toward the sounds of war. The explosions of cannons going off and their shells tearing up the earth grew louder. Rifle blasts also filled the air.

When the boys reached the outskirts of town, there were fifteen or twenty residents already there watching the battle. Being at ground level, they still had a hard time seeing anything. There were a few trees in the area, but townspeople had already climbed up them to get a better look. Darrell wanted to walk on farther, but Kenny's arm grabbed him and halted his progress.

"Darrell, we have to wait for Mr. Johnson," he said.

"Kenny, he ain't gonna make it up here—not unless his mouth gets tired of moving up and down so much. I just wanna get a little closer. We'll still be at a safe distance away from the battle. C'mon, Kenny. I swear we'll find a safe spot."

There wasn't much Kenny could do. When Darrell had a plan to do something, there was no stopping him. All Kenny could do was just go along silently with him. He sometimes hated following his friend into predicaments, but that was his lot in life—to follow after Darrell.

Darrell kept moving forward. Cannon blasts got louder and louder. Sounds of officers yelling to soldiers became audible. The number of Gettysburg residents alongside the boys had diminished to zero. They were out farther ahead than anyone else.

"Darrell, we're getting too close," Kenny begged.

"Just a little bit farther, Kenny. I think I see the perfect place," Darrell said. The war was drawing him closer and closer into its clutches.

Then Darrell saw it—a perfect place to safely watch the battle: a three-story brick building, and at its top was what looked like a bell tower without a bell in it. It was a cupola, where you could look out all over the whole area. The cupola was round and painted white with a green-domed roof with a large cross on its top. A sign in front of the building read Lutheran Theological Seminary.

"Let's go in there, Kenny. We can go all the way up to the top. I bet we can see really good up there!" Darrell yelled as he started off for the building.

When they got inside, they saw that the building was deserted. The boys figured that the first shots of war had probably scared everybody off. Darrell led Kenny up the stairs. He was really excited. Since 1861 he had been looking forward to witnessing the war. He had read every news article about it in the *Dubaville Times*. He had listened to all of Terry McIntyre's war stories. Now as he ran up the stairs and grasped the handle to the door leading to the top of the tower, he was finally going to see the war for himself. Darrell opened the door and stepped outside at the top of the cupola.

The two boys could see the entire battlefield. They could smell the heavy odor of gun smoke in the air. Darrell and Kenny saw the small cavalry unit clad in Union blue uniforms. They had dismounted from their horses and were dug in around a short wooden fence. They were bravely fighting the larger rebel force. It looked bad for the Union soldiers.

Just then, a large infantry regiment came advancing through town, past the building where the boys were watching the battle. The regiment was coming to reinforce the cavalry unit. The boys saw the soldiers marching smartly and began cheering. Some of the soldiers looked up and smiled at the boys as they passed the building where Darrell and Kenny were watching the battle. A few others doffed their hats in appreciation for the boys' applause.

"We're gonna win, Kenny!" Darrell shouted. "We're gonna be here to see General Lee take a whooping."

The reinforcements slammed into the Confederate army and drove them back into a wooded area. The boys saw a general on a horse commanding Union soldiers to the positions that they should take on the field. He rode up and down the line, encouraging the soldiers. As he was riding to where a new group of infantry had gathered, the boys saw a bullet strike the back of the general's head. The leader fell from his horse—dead before hitting the ground.

Watching the death of the Union general affected Darrell and Kenny. They had never seen anything like it before. Darrell knew soldiers died in war, but to witness such a brutal example of it caught him off guard.

"Darrell, I don't know if I want to be so close to the action to see people die like that general just did," Kenny said hesitantly.

"I'm sorta glad we're up here instead of fighting, Kenny. This is not what I expected war to be like at all."

After their leader went down, the Union soldiers became confused. A new general came running up to take the other one's place. He reorganized the soldiers as they renewed their assault on the Confederate army.

Soldiers on both sides stood and fired bullets into each other. The warriors weren't shooting at each other while hiding behind cover; they were out in the open.

The boys saw some soldiers get hit and fall to the ground with wounds to their heads or bodies. When they fell, the soldiers writhed in pain. They also saw other soldiers who fell to the ground and never moved again. First, there were a few soldiers. Then there were tens of wounded or dead soldiers. Soon the boys witnessed the death or wounding of hundreds of soldiers from both the Union side and the Confederate army. The field was scattered with bodies everywhere.

The Union army moved forward, lost a bunch of soldiers to Confederate fire, and then fell back to their original position. As Kenny watched the action, he turned to Darrell.

"Darrell, you never told me that war was like this," he said nervously. "They just stand there and get shot."

"I didn't know myself. I thought war would be great. I thought we could show up and be heroes without any problems. Terry McIntyre once told me how bloody war was, but I thought he was just trying to scare me. Now I see that he was right."

War wasn't glamorous and glorious as Darrell had thought. It was brutal and bloody, full of suffering and dying. The boys were getting an eyeful of the brutality. Darrell saw one soldier get shot in the arm. The bullet must have shattered the bone, because the arm just hung there with no movement. In fact, it looked as if the only thing keeping the soldier's arm attached to his body was the sleeve of his uniform. The soldier fell to the ground, yelling in pain. No one came to help him. A little while later, he didn't move around anymore.

Cannon fire began to add to the casualties. One cannonball exploded near a Union soldier. Fragments from the shell burst forward into the soldier and tore through him. Darrell looked the other way, and Kenny turned green at the sight.

"I don't think I want to stay here any longer, Darrell. I've seen too much!" Kenny pleaded.

"Kenny, I think we're gonna win the battle. Don't you want to see Bobby Lee lose?"

"I don't care about that anymore. I just wanna get outta here."

The boys saw a bunch of Confederate soldiers moving forward on the extreme right side of the battlefield. They were trying to break through the Union line. The boys saw that the Northern soldiers were hiding behind a stone fence that was built just for the battle. The Union soldiers waited for the Confederates to get close to the fence. The rebel soldiers had no way of knowing what they were about to walk into, but Darrell and Kenny could see it clearly from their position in the tower. All at once, the Union soldiers stood up and fired into the charging army. When the gun smoke cleared, there were only a few rebels left standing. They retreated to where they came from. The dead and wounded bodies were piled on top of each other. It was not war—it was slaughter.

"Did you see that?" Darrell yelled. "I told you we're gonna win!"

Kenny was horrified at seeing so many soldiers die at once. Even though they were soldiers from the other side, Kenny still felt bad for them. They were living, breathing human beings one minute, and dead soldiers the next. When Kenny ran away with Darrell to join the army, he thought it would be a fun adventure. Now it had turned into a nightmare. Kenny wanted the experience to end.

"Darrell, don't you think that we should get back to check on my aunt and Elizabeth?" Kenny said. "My aunt is probably worried about us."

"Kenny, we told your aunt that we'd stay in a safe place, away from the fighting—and we are in a safe place."

"Yeah, but we aren't with Mr. Johnson. I swear, Darrell, if you get me into trouble, General Lee won't be the only one getting whooped."

"Relax, Kenny. Just give me a few more minutes. If we haven't won by then, I'll go back to your aunt's house with you."

Darrell saw a large group of Confederate troops arriving to reinforce the enemy. Now they outnumbered the Union soldiers by more than two to one. He watched as they attacked all at once throughout the battlefield. The Union soldiers stood bravely and fought, but they were no match for the enormous gray-clad force. The Southerners didn't care that running out in the open made it easier for the Northern army to shoot them down; they had superior numbers, and there was no way the Union troops could stop so many of them. This fact soon became apparent to the Union soldiers, and they began to run in retreat. First just a few soldiers ran, and then Darrell saw large numbers of Union soldiers fleeing for their lives.

Darrell had been so sure his side was going to win that when he saw the Union army run he was surprised and disappointed. Kenny used the retreat as an opportunity to get Darrell to leave the battlefield.

"Darrell, we gotta get outta here!" he yelled to his friend. "The rebels will be on us in no time."

"I really thought this was the battle where we would finally beat ole Bobby Lee," Darrell said dejectedly. "I don't understand what happened."

"What happened is nobody beats General Lee. Now let's get outta here before the rebs arrive."

"Yeah, you're right. Let's go," Darrell sighed.

Soldiers were running past the building where Darrell and Kenny sat. There were generals shouting for the soldiers to stay and fight, but their orders fell on deaf ears. Soldiers who just minutes before were standing up to the Confederates were now running as fast as they could back through the streets of Gettysburg. It was time for the boys to get back to the McElroy house.

# Chapter 9

## KENNY'S DISTRESS

The Union soldiers were running from the battlefield. Some of them turned and shot their rifles as they retreated, and others simply ran as fast as they could toward the town of Gettysburg. Kenny had finally convinced Darrell that they should join the soldiers in their flight southward.

They were still in the tower when they saw a Union soldier coming toward their building. He looked like he was going to run right inside. Before reaching the front door, he turned to fire his rifle. Just as he was ready to fire, a bullet blasted into his chest, sending the soldier flying backward. He lay on his back. He looked up at the boys as they were looking down on him, and their glances locked. Darrell wanted do something to help him, but he didn't know what to do. The soldier pleaded with his eyes for someone to help him. Blood poured from his chest—already his dark blue uniform was soaked with the vital fluid of life.

"C'mon Darrell. We gotta get out of here," Kenny pleaded, snapping Darrell out of his thoughts.

"Do you think the soldier is trying to say something to us?" Darrell asked.

"Yeah, he's saying, 'Get outta here,'" Kenny lied. "Let's go!"

Darrell and Kenny ran down the steps to exit the building. When they got to the ground floor, they were in a large hallway. The door to the left exited to the rear of the building. The wounded soldier that the boys saw from the tower was lying on the ground just outside the door to the right. Kenny raced to the back door, opened it, and was ready to run out. He turned to see where Darrell was, and he could see that his friend was standing back near the stairway.

"Darrell, what are you doing? Come on!" he yelled.

Darrell didn't move. He kept staring at the front door. Kenny ran back to grab him and make him leave with him.

"Darrell, we gotta get out of here, now!"

"Kenny, do you think we should go and see if we can do something for the injured soldier out there?"

"Are you crazy? We don't know nothing about doctoring. Besides, if we open that door, we'll be the next ones lying on the ground with a bullet in us. Forget about him, and let's go!"

"Kenny, let's just go and try to help him for one minute. I swear—one minute. After that, we'll leave."

"What can you do? You're just gonna get us killed. You promised my aunt that we'd stay a safe distance away from the action. You go out that door, and we'll be right in the middle of it."

"I still think that we can help him. I don't wanna just leave him there to die," Darrell said.

"It's nice you wanna help him, but you don't know anything about what to do. I say let's just get outta here before the whole rebel army is swarming all over us."

Kenny's words just bounced off of Darrell. He didn't hear a thing. Once he had his mind set on doing something, he was going to do it. He had set his mind on going out that front door to help the soldier. He made his way in that direction. He opened the door, went outside, and left Kenny alone in the building.

Outside, the scene was chaos. Soldiers were yelling, gunfire was all around the area, and cannon balls were blasting everywhere. Darrell went over the wounded soldier and knelt by him. When he saw the soldier, he was shocked. The infantryman looked almost as young as he was. He was shot in the chest, and both of his hands were covering the wound. His hands were crimson red from the blood.

The door to the building opened again, and Kenny came out. He came over to the soldier with an angry look in his eyes.

"I don't know why I keep following you around, Darrell Stouffer. I think you're gonna get us both killed."

"What can I do for you?" Darrell asked the soldier, ignoring Kenny.

"I—I'm thirsty," the soldier said, barely audible.

Darrell found his canteen. He took his hand and gently propped the soldier's head up so that he could drink the water. The soldier gulped so fast that half of the water came splashing back out of his mouth and down the front of his uniform.

"There—you did something. Now can we get outta here?" Kenny pleaded.

"I don't wanna die," the soldier spoke, tears running down his cheeks. Darrell didn't say anything. He just looked at the soldier sympathetically.

Kenny bent over the soldier to get closer to Darrell and yelled, "Darrell, let's get outta here!"

All at once, the injured soldier grabbed Kenny's shirt. He pulled Kenny down to where his face was just inches away from his own.

"I said, I don't wanna die!" the soldier cried.

Kenny looked into the injured soldier's eyes. He wanted to break away, but the soldier had a tight grip on his shirt. The blood from his hands stained it. The soldier looked at Kenny for a second, and then he closed his eyes and did what he didn't want to do—he died. His hands still grasped Kenny's shirt.

Kenny just knelt there, looking into the dead soldier's face. Darrell frantically began trying to pry the dead soldier's hands away from Kenny's shirt. He worked feverishly, but the death grip the soldier had on his friend's shirt was tight.

When he finally had Kenny free, Kenny began to move back away from the soldier. Just then a bullet whizzed past Kenny's head. It came within a fraction of an inch from hitting him and ending his life. The bullet struck the wall behind the boys, sending fragments of brick on top of them.

That was the last straw. Kenny had been shocked all day by the brutality of war. He had watched the death of a soldier just inches from his face, and his shirt was discolored by the dead soldier's blood.

Now he had just come within a whisker of his own death. It was all too much for him. Something inside snapped—some light that made Kenny alive went out. He was sitting on the ground—alive, but not alive. What was inside of him wasn't working. He was in a state of shock.

Now it was Darrell's turn to plead to leave the area.

"Kenny, we gotta go. Come on!" Darrell yelled, but Kenny didn't move.

Darrell looked into Kenny's eyes. He could see that there was something wrong. He didn't know what had happened to his friend. He pleaded again for Kenny to get up, but Kenny didn't budge. Darrell grabbed his shoulders and tried to shake him awake. It didn't work; something had Kenny in its grips. Kenny was breathing—other than that, it was like he was dead. Darrell grabbed Kenny and pulled him up to his feet. Kenny just stood there with a blank stare.

"Kenny, what's wrong with you?" Darrell cried.

He shook him again, but it didn't do any good. All around the boys, Union soldiers were scurrying in retreat. Darrell knew he had to get Kenny out of there. But Kenny didn't move. Darrell pushed him, and Kenny stumbled forward, barely bending his knees.

Darrell had tears running down his face. *What have I done to him?* he asked himself.

Darrell was scared, but he was determined to save his friend.

He had to keep pushing Kenny to keep him moving. They were going slow, but at least they were heading in the right direction. Darrell was scared for his friend. This had all been his fault. If they had left when Kenny wanted to, Kenny wouldn't be like this.

*Why isn't he waking up?* Darrell wondered.

Darrell and Kenny passed the area north of town where the residents had gathered just hours before to watch the battle. Everyone had left the area. Darrell realized that they should have stayed with the citizens of Gettysburg—even with Mr. Johnson. If they had, they'd be safe now, and Kenny wouldn't be in his present condition of distress. He kept pushing Kenny forward, hoping that at some moment Kenny would snap out of it. But Kenny was still frozen in shock.

In town, confusion reigned. Union soldiers were running everywhere. Some of the wounded soldiers, deciding that they could go no further, knocked on residents' houses, begging the inhabitants to take them in. Most people responded positively, taking in the wounded soldiers. Other soldiers just kept running through town. Bullets hurtled overhead.

Darrell continued lugging Kenny through the streets. Every few steps he would plead for Kenny to wake up. He would shake him again and again, but whatever had Kenny in its clutches was not ready to let go of him.

Finally, they reached the McElroy residence. Darrell pushed Kenny inside the front door of the house. Inside, Aunt Clara and Elizabeth were huddled behind some furniture, scared from the noises that they heard from outside. Aunt Clara saw the blood on Kenny's shirt and screamed.

"Is he hurt?" she called to Darrell.

Darrell had forgotten about the blood on Kenny's shirt. "No, he didn't get shot. We stopped to help a wounded soldier, and he got his bloody hands on Kenny's shirt."

"What's wrong with him?" Aunt Clara cried.

"I don't know. He won't wake up. I keep shaking him and shaking him, but he won't wake up."

Aunt Clara sat Kenny down on a chair, and then she got a cloth and dampened it with water. She took the rag and patted Kenny's face. Then she dampened the cloth again and placed it on the back of Kenny's neck.

"Why didn't you boys come back when you were supposed to? We've been worried sick about you."

Darrell looked over at Elizabeth. She had a scared look on her face. Darrell felt even worse than before about what he had done to Kenny.

"It's all my fault. Kenny wanted to leave. We saw a soldier get hit with a bullet. I wanted to see if we could help him. Kenny kept begging to leave. I shoulda listened to him. I'm sorry, Mrs. McElroy. I'm sorry, Kenny. Can you hear me? I said, I'm sorry!"

The wet cloth on Kenny's neck and the calmness in the room began to help Kenny, and soon a little spark came back into his eyes. He finally began to wake up. Darrell had tears in his eyes as Kenny revived. Aunt Clara drew a sigh of relief.

"The bullet . . ." were Kenny's first words.

"It's all right, Kenny," Darrell said to his friend. "The bullet missed you. You're okay. You're gonna be okay!"

"What bullet?" Aunt Clara angrily demanded.

"When we stopped to help the soldier, a bullet came close to hitting Kenny, but it missed him," Darrell sheepishly remarked. He kept asking himself, *How could I have been so stupid?*

Kenny was alert again. With the end of Kenny's crisis, Aunt Clara turned her attention to the noises of war coming from outside.

"Darrell, what's going on out there?" Aunt Clara asked.

"The Union's on the run. The Confederates should be in town in no time," Darrell reported.

Darrell suddenly remembered that the McElroy's had a big garden. Last night at dinner, they ate beans freshly picked from it. If the Confederates came into town, they would be looking for whatever food that they could find. Someone was going to have to go out and pick what was ripe in the garden.

"Mrs. McElroy, we got to get whatever food that we can pick out of the garden. If we leave it there, the rebels will take everything."

With Elizabeth scared, and Kenny barely able to function, Aunt Clara had no time to go and pick vegetables.

"Darrell, will you go out there and get it? I'll stay in here and take care of Kenny and Elizabeth," Aunt Clara pleaded.

"Elizabeth—wanna help me?" Darrell asked.

"I'm too afraid to go out there," Elizabeth stuttered.

"Okay, you stay here and help Kenny," Darrell said. "I'll go out and get whatever I can."

Darrell picked up the laundry basket that Mrs. McElroy had used the previous day and headed out to the backyard. He picked everything that he could find—beans, strawberries, carrots, squash, and zucchini. Even if it wasn't quite ripe yet, Darrell picked it so that the Confederate army wouldn't find anything to eat in their garden. He hurried back inside.

"Here. Hide this. If the rebs come inside the house looking for food, you can't let them find it," ordered Darrell.

Elizabeth asked worriedly, "Do you think that they'll bust in here, Darrell?"

"I don't know, but just in case they do, we can't have anything that they might want lying around."

Mrs. McElroy walked over to Darrell. "How long do you think before the Confederates will be in town?"

"They're probably in the north side right now. Won't take 'em long to get down here," Darrell answered.

"Darrell, will you do me a favor? Will you go to the store and bring back my husband?" Aunt Clara implored. "Please. If the enemy soldiers go into the store and Levi is there, I'm afraid that he'll try to protect his goods. They might kill him. Darrell—please go and bring him home!"

Darrell looked over at Kenny, and then at Elizabeth. With her eyes, Elizabeth was pleading to Darrell to go get her father. Kenny was finally up and walking on his own, but he was in no shape to go back out into the war. He hadn't said anything since he first snapped out of the shock that had paralyzed him. Darrell was going to have to do this on his own.

"Okay. You all stay here. Kenny, you help protect the women. I'll be right back," Darrell said, and then off he went out the door.

The situation outside had gotten even worse than before. Union soldiers were lying in the streets—some dead, others crying for help. Darrell saw a Confederate soldier working his way down the road. He looked like he was ready to shoot anything that moved. Darrell quickly turned down a side street to avoid him. Rifles kept firing, men kept shouting, and the wounded kept wailing. It was hell on earth, and Darrell was running right into the middle of it.

At last, Darrell arrived at the McElroy store. Inside, Uncle Levi was in the process of trying to hide items that he thought the Confederate army might want.

"What are you doing here?" he demanded bluntly when he saw Darrell.

"Mr. McElroy, your wife and Elizabeth need you to come home. Please, let's go," Darrell pleaded.

"I can't. Who'll protect this place if I'm home?"

"You can't protect it, Mr. McElroy. There's too many rebels out there. Your wife needs you. You gotta come home with me to protect your family."

Uncle Levi thought for a moment. He looked around the store and just saw stuff. What he had at home was more precious than a bunch of junk. Darrell was right. He needed to be with his family—not worrying about some silly store.

"Just a minute," he said. He went off and brought back a rifle and some ammunition to help protect his family.

Remembering the look on the rebel soldier whom he saw on the way to the store, Darrell said, "Mr. McElroy, you can't bring that rifle. The rebels are already in town. If they see you with that gun, they might think that you're a Union soldier and open fire on you. You gotta leave it behind."

"You're right," Uncle Levi said. He took the rifle and put it behind the counter. Then he came over to Darrell and said, "Let's go."

Darrell and Uncle Levi began running through the streets. The same chaotic scene that Darrell had witnessed on his trip to the store reigned on his trip back home. The two turned the corner, and there were three Confederate soldiers. Seeing movement, all three of the soldiers brought their guns up and aimed them directly at Darrell and Uncle Levi. The two stopped, frozen in fright.

Darrell thought about the dying soldier's last words—"I don't wanna die"—and realized that those might be his last words as well. The soldiers were mean-looking with wrinkled uniforms that had once been colored gray but were now a filthy brownish color from not being washed. The three looked as if they hadn't shaved in a few days; stubble covered their faces.

Darrell was grateful that he had talked Uncle Levi out of carrying the rifle. They would have been dead for sure if the three rebels had spotted a firearm. The three soldiers, seeing that two civilians had caused the commotion, lowered their rifles. One of the soldiers made a movement with his head, indicating that Darrell and Uncle Levi should leave. He didn't have to nod twice. The two were off and running in no time.

Darrell and Uncle Levi reached the McElroy house in minutes and burst through the front door. Elizabeth ran and threw her arms around her father. She was crying tears of joy that her father had made it home. Aunt Clara joined the family hug. She was happy that her husband was safe. While still hugging her father, Elizabeth looked at Darrell and smiled.

"Thank you, Darrell," she said.

That little bit of tenderness was what Darrell needed. The day had been so savage. That little smile from Elizabeth did wonders to help wash away the brutality. Darrell felt good that he could elicit that small token of gratitude from Elizabeth.

"You're welcome," was all that he could get out of his mouth. What he really wanted to say was, "I love you." After such a terrible day, he didn't care what Kenny or anybody else would say if they knew that he liked Elizabeth. He had to reveal his feelings to Elizabeth the first chance he could get. He would have to take the chance that she might say that she didn't feel the same way about him.

Uncle Levi began to take charge in the house. He looked at Kenny and was as shocked as Aunt Clara had been to see the blood on his shirt. Kenny was okay again, but he didn't want to talk about the things that he had seen that day. Uncle Levi talked to Darrell about the events of the battle.

"I thought for a long time that we were gonna win," Darrell said.

"I don't know if it is over yet," Uncle Levi responded. "Dave Redunski said that the Union soldiers were reforming on a hill south of town by the cemetery. I think we might have some more fighting before we're through."

Darrell took heart with this latest revelation. Maybe the Union army could still defeat General Lee after all. This was just the first day of fighting. The South might have won today, but it's the final battle that counts.

That night, Darrell and Kenny went to bed early. Kenny was exhausted and still recovering from his shock. Darrell apologized again in the bedroom, but Kenny didn't want to be reminded about the events of the day. The light knock on the door let both boys know that Elizabeth was coming to visit again.

"Are you guys okay?" she asked.

"Yeah," Darrell said.

"I was so scared today. Ever since we heard the gunshots in the morning, I've been on edge. I know the rebels are in town, but at least the firing has stopped."

"It'll be okay, Elizabeth," Darrell said, trying to console her. "Your dad said that the Union troops have moved south of town. Any more fighting is probably gonna happen there. We're safe in town."

"I hope so," Elizabeth sighed. "You okay, Kenny? You've hardly said two words since you got back."

"I don't wanna talk about it," was all Kenny said.

"That's okay. You just rest and take it easy. I'll leave you two boys alone."

Darrell walked Elizabeth to the door. His heart was pounding so hard, he was sure that she could hear it. He had to tell her how he felt about her. Elizabeth turned back and looked at Darrell.

"Thanks again for bringing home my father." She reached down and grasped his hand. She had that same tender smile that she had had on her face earlier. Darrell wanted to say something, but when she grabbed his hand, the words froze in his mouth. He knew he was head-over-heels in love with Elizabeth—now he had to find a way to tell her. But just as he mustered up some courage, Elizabeth turned and left the room, leaving Darrell alone with his heavy feeling.

*There's always tomorrow,* he thought.

# Chapter 10

# THE FIELD HOSPITAL

The Confederate army had invaded the town of Gettysburg. The soldiers took food from citizens and from stores. Sometimes they knocked on people's doors and asked for food, and other times they crashed through the doors and demanded it. With the commotion from outside that night, sleep was not easy in the McElroy home. There was sporadic shooting here and there, but mostly what was heard were the Confederates shouting to one another.

After Darrell and Kenny went to bed, all Darrell could think about was what Uncle Levi had said. The Northern army was on the hills south of town, and there would be a battle on Thursday. He replayed the first day of the battle over and over in his mind. He had been sure the Union army would win the day, and he was bitterly disappointed to see the army run in retreat. But what if Uncle Levi was correct? The Union army might still have a chance to redeem themselves the following day.

Darrell got up before the sun rose. He was hoping to sneak out of the house, past the Southern lines, and investigate where the Union army was. He was also hoping to find a place where he could safely watch the action of the second day of the battle. After witnessing so many soldiers die on the battlefield the previous day, he had decided that it would be safer to watch the fighting rather than take part in it.

As he got up, he saw Kenny sleeping. Darrell did not want to wake him. Kenny was still shook up over what had happened on the previous day, and Darrell knew that he wouldn't want to go back to the battlefield to witness another day of fighting. Darrell quietly dressed by himself.

To Darrell's amazement, Kenny woke up on his own. He was usually a very sound sleeper. When Kenny awoke and saw Darrell getting dressed, he started to sleepily do the same. Darrell was shocked. He didn't think that there was any way that he could convince Kenny to come watch the second day's battle with him, and yet, there he was dressing himself without Darrell even asking. He didn't want to say anything to Kenny for fear that he would wake up everyone else in the house. So he decided that he would talk to his friend when they got outside.

Both of the boys got dressed, went downstairs, and grabbed a handful of cookies from the counter to serve as a quick breakfast. They quietly exited the back door of the house. Outside they had to be careful. Confederate soldiers were everywhere, and noise might just bring a rifle shot in their direction.

"Kenny, I'm so surprised at you," Darrell quietly said to his friend. "I didn't think that you would go with me to watch today's battle, but here you are!"

"I ain't going with you," Kenny answered. "I'm going home."

"What did you say?" Darrell responded confused.

"I said, I ain't going with you. I'm going home."

"C'mon Kenny. I said I was sorry about yesterday. I won't put you in a bad place today. We'll find a really safe place to watch the fighting, and when you want to leave, I promise I'll leave with you."

"Darrell, I ain't no soldier. I don't know what I'm doing here. I'm a farmer. I should be in my cornfield. That's exactly where I'm heading."

"But you can't go home. We haven't seen old Bobby Lee take his lumps yet. I just know we'll eventually win. Stay and watch—just today. If we don't win the battle today, I'll go home with you tomorrow."

"I saw too much yesterday. I dreamt about it all last night. Maybe I'll dream about watching that boy die every night for the rest of my life. You like this stuff—I don't. I don't belong here. I should be back home working the fields and helping my father. Darrell, I don't wanna see or hear anything more of this war. If we're still fighting General Lee when I turn eighteen, well then, maybe I'll think about joining up. Until then, I'm staying home."

"But, Kenny, we're a team. We do everything together. You gotta stay—at least stay here at your uncle's house. I'll let you know what happens in the battle today."

"We're not a team, Darrell," Kenny said matter-of-factly. "I always do what you want to do. I stay as long as you want to stay. I think that from here and now, I'm gonna do what I wanna do, and what I wanna do is go home."

Darrell looked at Kenny. He looked so sure of his decision. It used to be so easy to make Kenny feel guilty for not going along with what he wanted him to do. But Kenny looked different this morning. He looked determined. This was not the Kenny he had grown up with. Maybe all the things that happened yesterday had forced Kenny to grow up. Darrell tried one last time to convince his friend to stay in Gettysburg.

"C'mon Kenny. I don't want you to go. What am I gonna do here? These are your folks—they're not mine. If you go, then I'll have to go."

"No you don't. My aunt and uncle like you a lot. They'll let you stay here with 'em. You don't have to go with me. You stay here and get whatever hold this war has on you out of your system. When you come home, I'll teach you how to love farming."

Darrell knew that there was no way to change Kenny's mind. For the first time in his life, Kenny was standing up to him. The only thing that he could do was wish him the best and go on by himself.

"Kenny, you take care going home. You're likely to run into the whole Confederate army heading back to Dubaville," Darrell said, finally giving in.

"They can't catch me. I'll sneak right past them old rebels. You take it easy yourself. When you reach the Union side, there'll probably be Northern soldiers out there who'll shoot anything they see moving."

"I'm hoping most of them'll be asleep," Darrell confided.

"I'll stop by your house and let your mom and dad know that you're all right. I'll tell 'em that you ain't gonna fight—you're just gonna watch. Now don't go doing something stupid like getting your head blown off!"

"I won't. Thanks, Kenny!"

Darrell held out his hand. Kenny shook it. Their friendship had moved to a new level. They were both equals now. In a way, Darrell liked the new Kenny better than the old one. He was more sure of himself. Darrell respected that. The boys turned in different directions to depart. Suddenly, Kenny called out to Darrell.

"Darrell, before you go I gotta tell you something. But you gotta swear you'll never say anything about it to anyone. It's a secret told to me that I'm not supposed to tell you. Promise me you won't say anything."

Darrell was intrigued with Kenny's secret. He'd promise not to tell, but after hearing the secret, he would decide whether or not he would keep that promise.

"My cousin Elizabeth made me promise I wouldn't tell you. Darrell, Elizabeth likes you a lot. She thinks you're good-looking, nice, and very brave. She's real sweet on you. Now don't go telling her I told you this, or the next time I come to Gettysburg, she'll come after me."

"I promise—I won't say anything. Good luck, Kenny, and take care of yourself."

"You stay out of the way of them passing bullets, you hear? I hope you find whatever it is that you came to Gettysburg to find. C'mon home just as soon as you can."

With that, the two boys parted ways. Darrell's head was swimming with Kenny's secret. So Elizabeth liked him. Telling her that he liked her was going to be easy now. He didn't have to worry about how she would react. He already knew how she felt about him. Darrell had to keep his mind on moving around the Confederate soldiers, but it was hard. Elizabeth had said that she liked him. That was the best news he had heard in a long time. The uneasy feeling he had the night before when he was struggling to tell Elizabeth his feelings was gone. He was happy—the girl that he liked had said that she liked him.

Getting past the Southern soldiers in town wasn't very hard for Darrell. They mostly gathered on the main streets, leaving side roads empty. There was no one standing guard and looking for residents who might be wandering around. It was still dark, and the small fires that the soldiers were burning didn't reveal very much a few feet beyond their flames.

Getting past the Union sentries south of town was another thing. They were constantly on alert for the slightest movement, and they were eager to fire their rifles at anything that they thought that they saw. Darrell moved very slowly past these sentries, and then went behind the Union lines. He wanted to see a campsite and maybe scope out a safe place to watch the day's fighting. The sun was just peaking over the horizon, but it was still pretty dark. Darrell kept walking behind the Northern lines to see what was there.

As he was walking, he saw a line of big tents far ahead of him. There were campfires near each of the tents. He decided that this would be a good place to look around. As he got a little closer, he could see a man in front of one of the tents, sitting in a chair. Darrell moved closer and closer. He noticed that the man was slouched over. Was he alive, or was he dead? Darrell couldn't quite figure it out.

As Darrell drew near, he noticed that the man had some kind of long apron on over the front of his uniform. The apron had a big dirty splotch in the front. When Darrell walked closer to the man, he noticed that the dirty spot wasn't really dirt—it was blood. There was a huge area of blood on the slouched soldier's apron. Darrell stopped a second to look at the man. The blood reminded him of the soldier that they watched die the day before. Seeing the man in the chair saddened him. Death was a part of war that he had never really thought of.

Once he got past the soldier in the chair, he headed for the big tent that was behind him. Darrell thought that if he looked inside the tent, he would see a whole bunch of sleeping soldiers—the tent was so large. But when he looked inside the tent, all he saw was a big, long table with a bunch of tools on top of it. *What is this table for?* Darrell wondered.

He decided to keep looking around to see if he could find some soldiers. He walked behind the tent that he had just looked into. There Darrell saw a pile of something that reeked with a rotten odor. When he got nearer to the pile, he stopped dead in his tracks. Right ahead of him was a mass of body parts. There were arms and legs and feet and hands all piled on top of each other. It was the most horrible thing he had ever seen. The body parts were all bloody, and the blood was dripping to the ground and spreading downhill. Darrell looked down at his shoes and saw that he was standing in a puddle of the blood.

The scene was too much for him. He screamed at the top of his lungs, turned, and ran as fast as he could away from the grisly sight. As he ran, Darrell was looking back, and he wasn't watching where he was going. Suddenly . . . *SLAM!* . . . something stopped his forward movement. He looked up to see what he had run into, and again, he was aghast. It was the soldier with the bloody apron. He had come back to life! Darrell started to scream a second time, but the soldier took his big hand and muffled the sound.

"What are you doing back here?" he commanded.

"I—I—I was just looking around. I didn't mean to do anything wrong," Darrell was able to say when the big man took his hand away from Darrell's mouth.

"Who are you?" the man questioned.

"I'm Darrell—Darrell Stouffer, sir," he somehow managed to say. The soldier looked at Darrell and saw that he was just a young boy.

"My name is Captain Stephen Robinson," the soldier told Darrell in a voice that wasn't as harsh as before. "I'm a surgeon with the Army of the Potomac. You really shouldn't be back here. You should be home."

"I just wanted to look around. Can I ask you a question, sir?" Darrell asked.

"Sure. What is it?"

"That pile back there . . . what is it?"

"Oh, that's what's got you hollering. You see, as a surgeon, my job is to keep as many of our wounded boys alive after a battle as is possible. You see this?" Captain Robinson put his hand in his pocket and pulled out a small, cone-shaped bullet made of lead. "This is what we call a minié ball. It's what the soldiers fire out of their rifles."

Darrell held the ball in his hand. "It's really light," he told Captain Robinson.

Captain Robinson took the minié ball back and began moving it toward Darrell's arm as if simulating that it had been fired at him.

"You see, if this ball is fired into your arm," Captain Robinson pressed the ball into Darrell's arm just above the elbow, "it will shatter the bone. When you're brought to me for surgery, there isn't much I can do other than amputate or cut off the damaged part of your arm. There are so many wounded soldiers, that I don't have time to properly deal with your amputated body part. So I just throw it on a pile, and I go on to the next wounded soldier. I'll have someone come along later this morning and bury that pile of limbs. There's gonna be another fight later, and I'll probably make another pile that size or maybe even bigger."

"Is that why your apron's all bloody—from the operating?" Darrell asked.

"Yeah, I was too tired to take it off after my last operation," Captain Robinson said.

"Where are all the soldiers you operated on yesterday?" Darrell asked.

"Out there, behind you in the field."

The sun had risen to a point where you could dimly see objects, and when Darrell turned around, he was shocked to see a large group of wounded soldiers. There were well over fifty soldiers lying in the grass. They all had some part of their body wrapped in bloody bandages. As the soldiers began waking up, many cried out in pain. Darrell wondered how he could have missed seeing the soldiers when he was walking up to the camp earlier—there were so many of them.

"Are they all from yesterday's battle?" Darrell asked.

"Yeah, and I bet there are still some more out there on the battlefield that haven't been brought back to me yet."

"I saw that battle yesterday," Darrell stated. "For a while there I thought that they were gonna win, and then the soldiers ran in defeat."

"Those boys fought bravely against a larger army. They retreated to where they are today, which I hear is a pretty strong line of defense. They deserve a lot of credit for their action yesterday. When I operate on each soldier, I remember the sacrifice that he has given for his country. I do my best to give him the best medical treatment. Those are brave boys out there in that field."

Captain Robinson spoke in a way that made Darrell feel honored to talk with him. He had an aura of authority as well as a genuine respect for the soldiers he helped. Darrell began to feel that same feeling that Captain Robinson had about the soldiers. He would no longer complain about their retreat from the previous day.

"Say, are you from around here, Darrell?" Captain Robinson inquired.

"Yeah, from pretty close around here," Darrell responded.

"Do you know where there's a creek where I can get some water?"

"Sure. I passed one as I was making my way to this camp from town. It's not far from here," Darrell answered, feeling good that he might be able to help Captain Robinson.

Captain Robinson looked around the field. He saw a soldier walking sleepily about twenty yards away. He called out to him. "Private. Come here!"

The soldier stopped walking and looked toward where the voice came from. Once he realized that it was from an officer, he ran as fast as he could toward Captain Robinson. When he arrived, he stiffened up his body and saluted the officer.

"Private Morris. This is Darrell Stouffer. He knows where a creek is. Get a bunch of canteens, follow Darrell, and get some water for the wounded boys. It's gonna be another hot day today, and we're gonna need to get some water into them soon," Captain Robinson commanded.

"Yes, sir," replied Private Morris.

He saluted Captain Robinson again and then turned to Darrell. "C'mon, kid. Follow me," he said, and then started walking toward another tent. Darrell followed him.

When they reached the tent, Darrell saw a bunch of canteens on the ground. Before picking any of them up, Private Morris turned to Darrell.

"My name's Private Jimmy Morris. You can just call me Jimmy if you want," he said, and held out his hand for Darrell to shake. Jimmy Morris was young—maybe eighteen years old. He had a friendly smile. Jimmy was about the same size as Darrell, but he was solid, as if he had worked hard all of his life.

Darrell shook his hand and introduced himself. "Hi, Private Morris. I'm Darrell Stouffer." Darrell wanted to treat Private Morris like a soldier. He would not call him Jimmy.

"You from around here?" Private Morris asked.

"Yeah, pretty close." Darrell and the soldier began picking up canteens. When each of them had eight or nine, they headed off in the direction of the creek.

"Is it always this hot around here? I can't stand the humidity."

"Yeah," Darrell answered. "It gets hot around here in June, and it don't cool down till September."

"I'm from Michigan, myself. Lansing, Michigan. It might get hot there for a day or two, but then it cools off right away. Between the heat of Virginia and Gettysburg—I can't wait to get home and feel some cool air again."

Darrell really liked Private Morris. He didn't treat him like a kid, and he was really friendly.

"Did you fight in the battle yesterday?" Darrell asked.

"No. I don't fight. I'm in what we call the ambulance corp. You see, after the battle's over, it's up to me to run out to the battlefield and tend to the wounded. I bring them as fast as I can back to Captain Robinson or one of the other doctors who operates on 'em. We have a bunch of field hospitals set up in the area to help the wounded soldiers."

Darrell was a little disappointed. He thought that Private Morris was a real soldier. He was discouraged to find out that he didn't fight in the war. "Did you ever fight in a battle?" Darrell asked, hoping that there was some major reason why Private Morris wasn't out there trying to shoot rebels.

"Yeah. I used to be a regular soldier. I fought in Fredericksburg. Ole General Burnside kept sending us up a hill to try to beat Bobby Lee. It was a slaughter. Them rebs kept picking us off left and right. We had so many dead and wounded on that hill. When the fighting stopped, I started helping to take care of some of them. Captain Robinson saw how good I was at taking care of the hurt soldiers that he had me transferred to the ambulance corp. At first I didn't like it—I signed up to be a fighting soldier. Then I saw that I could make a difference in the lives of the soldiers who were injured, and now I like what I'm doing. I gotta say, so do my parents. When they learned that I wasn't in the line of fire anymore, they were relieved."

Darrell led Private Morris to a creek. The water was cool, but its level had receded down the side of the creek banks because of a lack of rain. The two began filling up the canteens with water.

"Did you ever wish you could go back to fighting in the war?" Darrell asked as they were working.

"Yeah. When we were at Chancellorsville, Stonewall Jackson was hitting us pretty hard. We fought him off for a little bit, and then we turned and ran in retreat. Before we left the field, I wanted to help out. Then I began to think about who would help the wounded if something ever happened to me. I stayed out of the battle and took care of the wounded after it was over. Maybe someday I'll pick up a rifle again, though."

Private Morris picked up half of the canteens and motioned for Darrell to grab the other half.

"Are you gonna be a doctor like Captain Robinson?" Darrell asked.

"Nah, I wanna be a lawyer once this war is over. I was applying to colleges before the war broke out. I wanna get back to my studies once it's over. You know, after the battle of Fredericksburg, I met this colonel from Pennsylvania. He was checking on his wounded soldiers. The two of us sat down for a long conversation. He was a lawyer from a place called Erie before the war. He had graduated from Harvard, and he promised to help me get into law school there once this war ends. Do you know what you wanna be when you get older?"

"I don't know. I guess I'll be a farmer like my father, but I don't know if I really wanna be a farmer," Darrell answered.

"Don't worry," Private Morris said. "You're young yet. You got lots of time to figure it out."

Then the two of them took their canteens and started back to the field hospital. Their long day of work had just begun.

# Chapter 11

## DARRELL'S DISTRESS

Private Morris and Darrell arrived back at camp just after the sun had risen above the horizon. The morning sun brought with it the dreaded combination of heat and humidity, which, combined with the pains of their injuries, made the plight of the wounded soldiers lying in the field even more miserable. As the soldiers began to awaken, they increased the volume of their moans of pain. Just a day before, these soldiers were healthy, vibrant men, fighting an aggressive enemy. Now most of them were weakened warriors, with one or two of their limbs amputated.

Private Morris prepared to deliver the water in the canteens to his injured comrades. He broke out some small, wafer-like crackers that the soldiers called hard tack. Most of the soldier preferred eating hard tack with coffee, which they would dunk the brittle biscuits in to soften them up. The problem was that there wasn't any coffee; the soldiers would have to chomp through the stale, old hard tack with their teeth.

"Hey, Darrell," he called out. "Wanna help?"

"What do I have to do?" Darrell queried.

"Take some canteens and some of this hard tack and go help the wounded soldiers. Let them have a good, long drink of water. It's really gonna get hot today, and we have to keep them hydrated. Talk with them. Most of them wanna talk about their families. Others will want to talk about how they were wounded yesterday. Stay and listen to them for a bit. Do you think you can do that?"

"Sure," Darrell said. He was happy to be helping; it felt like he was a part of the army.

He grabbed some of the hard tack biscuits and walked to a nearby soldier. He was tall, thin, and had blond hair. The soldier was ghostly pale. He was sweating a great deal. Darrell had never seen anyone sweat so much. The soldier's uniform was soaked with perspiration. He was breathing heavily, as if he had just finished running a long distance. As Darrell approached him, he noticed that the soldier's right arm had been amputated six inches above the elbow. His stub of an arm was wrapped in a bandage that was turning red from his blood. Darrell didn't want to look at the wound, so he knelt down on the soldier's left side.

"Hi, I'm Darrell Stouffer," he said. "Here, do you wanna drink?"

Before saying anything, the soldier grabbed the canteen and began gulping down the water. He slurped so quickly, that the water ran down his chin and soaked his chest. He drank so fast that he started coughing like he was choking a little bit. Darrell had to help the soldier, and after he had a good long drink, Darrell had to pry the canteen from him. There were many soldiers that needed water. This soldier couldn't take a whole canteen's worth. Finally the soldier relaxed a little.

"Thanks, kid," the soldier said when he had finished drinking. "My name's Private Garrett Jones. I'm from Akron, Ohio. You ever hear of it?"

"Not really," Darrell answered. "Is it nice there?"

"Yeah, I really miss it. I wish I was back home now."

"I'm sure they'll send you back home as soon as your arm heals up a little bit more," Darrell responded.

"I got me a girl back in Ohio. Her name is Rosanna Sherwood. You wanna see a picture of her?" Garrett offered. He handed Darrell a small photograph. The black and white picture was of a very pretty girl in a long dress.

"She's really pretty," Darrell told Private Jones.

"Yeah. She wanted to get married before I went off to war, but I said no. I didn't want her to turn into an army widow. Maybe I should have married her. It's too late now. I ain't never gonna see her again."

"Sure you will," Darrell encouraged, trying to help get Private Jones's spirit up. The soldier continued to breathe heavily and sweat excessively.

"I was so stupid. When I turned eighteen, I decided that I wanted to go and fight for my country. Lots of boys from Akron had already enlisted. I thought that if I went away to war I'd get all kinds of medals. Then maybe Rosie's family would be so proud of me. Her father don't like me so much. I don't know why."

Darrell was taken aback by what Private Jones had just said. He had run away from home for the same reason that Garrett had stated—to win medals. Darrell wondered if he had fought in yesterday's battle like he had wanted to, if he would've ended up like Garrett—all alone, on the verge of death.

"This is my first battle since I joined up, and it's also my last one. I think Rosie would've been happier if I stayed at home. She didn't care what her father thought about me. I guess it don't matter now. I ain't gonna make it through the day."

"Private Jones, you gotta stop talking like that. Captain Robinson's a good doctor. He's gonna keep you alive."

"You know what I wish?" Private Jones asked. "I wish I lived in another time—a time when there weren't no war between the states. Then me and Rosie would've got married, and I would've worked with my dad in his lumber business." He paused for a few seconds and then asked, "Will you do me a favor, Darrell?"

"Sure, anything. You just name it," Darrell replied.

Private Jones handed the picture of Rosanna back to Darrell. "Flip it over on the back side. That's Rosie's address. Promise you'll write to her for me. Tell her I loved her, and that my last thoughts were of her. Will you do that for me?"

"Private Jones. You're gonna get better. You can write that letter to her yourself," Darrell replied nervously. He had watched a soldier die the previous day, and he didn't want to witness another one pass away so soon afterward.

"Promise me!" Private Jones snapped. The forcefulness of his voice took Darrell by surprise. He decided that to get Private Jones calmed down that he would tell him that he would write to his girlfriend.

"Okay, I promise that I'll write her, but I think you're gonna be able to do it yourself."

When Private Jones heard that Darrell would write Rosanna, he laid his head down in the grass and smiled.

"Thanks, Darrell. Remember, tell her I was thinking of her when I died." Private Jones closed his eyes and smiled. Then he took one last breath and expired.

Darrell looked at Private Jones, and suddenly his body began to shake. The soldier's death deeply affected him. He had gone off to war for the same reasons that Darrell had wanted to go off to war. Darrell thought that war was supposed to be glorious and filled with honor. Instead he found out that it was ugly and filled with death.

Tears began to stream down his cheeks. Maybe his father was right—he was too young to go off to war. Maybe Kenny was right—they had seen too much horror not to be permanently affected by the bloodshed of war. What was he doing there? He didn't belong among the wounded. He had never cried so hard before. It was all too much to take in and not be upset.

Suddenly he couldn't breathe. He gulped air, but it wouldn't go down into his lungs. His body was burning like it was on fire—it needed oxygen. He decided to drop the canteens and the hard tack and start running. Maybe the physical exertion would force air into his lungs. He began running as fast as he could. He closed his eyes and threw his head back. Still no oxygen seemed to work its way to his lungs.

Captain Robinson saw Darrell running across the field. He went over to find out what was wrong. Captain Robinson grabbed Darrell by the arm, stopping him.

"Darrell! What happened?" Captain Robinson asked.

"He—he died. He looked at me, he smiled, and then he was dead," Darrell blurted out.

Captain Robinson looked at Darrell. He had forgotten that Darrell was still a boy. Darrell was tall—close to six feet in height. Because of his size, it was easy to mistake him for being older than he was. But seeing him now, with tears in his eyes, Captain Robinson got a better sense of how truly young Darrell was.

"Darrell, how old are you?" he asked.

"I'm thirteen," Darrell answered. "I just wanna get outta here, Captain Robinson. Please, let me go."

"Darrell, try to relax," Captain Robinson calmly told Darrell. "I guess this is my fault. I didn't realize how young you were." His soothing voice helped calm Darrell down enough to breathe normally again. "It's a hard thing seeing someone die. I don't blame you for running away from it."

"Captain Robinson, I don't wanna go back there where the wounded soldiers are."

"Okay, but before you go, let me tell you a story. You see, before the war, I was a doctor in Philadelphia. I took care of some of the finest families there. In fact, I come from a very rich family myself. When the war started, I was asked to be a surgeon. I didn't want to go at first. I had a good practice, and I made a whole lot more money than I do as an army surgeon."

"What made you change your mind?" Darrell asked.

"My father was an officer in the War of 1812. He talked me into joining the army. I originally enlisted for only six months. I figured that would be long enough to please him. That was back in 1861."

"How come you're still in the army, then? 1861 is a lot longer than six months ago. Do you really like being a doctor in the army?"

"Not at first," Captain Robinson said. "I was there after the first battle of Bull Run. I had so many soldiers to operate on that I didn't know what to do. There were all kinds of wounds that I had never seen in my practice back in Philly. I had never amputated anything before, and then I was thrown into a situation where I had to operate continuously for over twenty-four hours straight, taking off arms and legs. I decided that once my six months were over, I would hurry back to my practice in Philadelphia."

Darrell listened to Captain Robinson's story, but he was also still thinking about Private Garrett Jones. He had decided that he was never going back to help the wounded soldiers again. He didn't want to watch another soldier die.

"When the army fought again, I decided to go down to the battlefield to watch the action," Captain Robinson continued. "I saw the soldiers walk up to their death like you or I walk up to the dinner table. They showed no fear. I looked at my job—maybe I had to work for long periods of time, but at least I didn't have to worry about bullets or cannonballs hitting me. These boys risked their lives every day. There is honor in what they do. I made up my mind right then and there to stay in the army until the war was over. I was going to do my best to save as many lives as I could. The brave soldiers deserved my best efforts."

"But what about when they die? You can't save everybody," Darrell interrupted. "That boy just looked at me, smiled, and then he was dead. Just like the soldier that my friend Kenny and I saw yesterday. He was alive one minute—dead the next. I can't take watching any more of them die."

"Yeah, and that's hard to get used to," Captain Robinson answered. "But one thing you have to understand about war is that soldiers are gonna die. No matter how hard I try, I still can't save every one of them. I had to develop a thick skin. I have to do what I can for as many of them as possible and not get too upset over the ones that I can't save."

"I don't know if I can do that," Darrell said, trying to lay the groundwork to let Captain Robinson know that he wasn't going to go back to help the wounded.

"Darrell, you're young. What is being asked of you would make the oldest of us cringe. But look out there at the field of wounded soldiers. Most of them woke up this morning without an arm or a leg that they had when they woke up yesterday morning. They need someone to bring them some water and something to eat, and they need someone to just listen to them."

Darrell thought about Captain Robinson's words. Although he didn't want to witness another soldier die, he did like the idea of helping the wounded soldiers.

"You may not think that you did anything important for that soldier who just died, but you helped him a whole lot. During his final moments on Earth, he had someone to talk to. There he was, miles from home, but he didn't die alone. He had a friend with him at the end. He had you."

"I never thought of it that way," Darrell said.

"Darrell, I'm asking you to try to go back and help the soldiers. They need you to help them make it through the next few hours. Later, the ambulances will take them away to local barns or churches or people's houses where they can get better attention. I'm gonna need that field for today's wounded. Do you think you can do it, Darrell? No one will blame you if you say no, but we can sure use your help."

"I'll try, Captain Robinson," Darrell said. "I'm still scared of another one dying in front of me."

"If you think someone's gonna die, call me or Private Morris, and one of us will come over right away and be with the soldier until he passes. That way you don't have to be there when another soldier dies. Thanks for helping out, Darrell. I know that the soldiers will appreciate your efforts," Captain Robinson said, and then patted Darrell on the back as they walked back to the wounded soldiers.

Darrell went back to the spot where Private Garrett Jones had died. He had to pick up the canteens and the hard tack. When he got there, the body had already been removed. The only hint that Private Jones had been there was the fact that the grass that was matted down where his body had laid. Darrell picked up his things and began to move to the next soldier. He closed his eyes and said a little prayer.

"Please, God. Don't let this next soldier die on me. Please keep him alive!"

The next soldier that he came to was nothing like Private Jones. He actually smelled the soldier long before he got to him. His body odor was really bad. He was the dirtiest man Darrell had ever laid his eyes on. His skin was dirty, his uniform was filthy, and his hair was so greasy that Darrell was surprised that his head wasn't sitting in a big pool of oil from his hair. He had a long, brown-and-gray beard that was matted and tangled. As Darrell approached, the man smiled. He had maybe four teeth left in his mouth, and Darrell was certain they were rotting by the minute.

Still, there was something about the man that put Darrell at ease. He didn't look like he was going to die at any minute. He wasn't pale like Private Jones had been. The man's skin was a sun-beaten tan color. The soldier held his hand out for Darrell to shake. It was filthy, and he had long fingernails that had dirt encrusted between the fingernails and on the tops of the fingers. Darrell shook the man's hand, but then felt an urge to want to wash his hand quickly afterward.

"Howdy, boy!" the man jovially cried out. "Name's Jedediah Washburn, but y'all can call me Jed."

"Hi, Jed," Darrell nervously said. "My name's Darrell. Do you want some water?"

Jed took the canteen and began drinking. Darrell decided to let him have all of the water in the canteen. He was so dirty that he didn't want the next soldier to get any germs from Jedediah. He looked at Jed and saw that his right leg had been amputated. He figured Captain Robinson probably would have had to wash the area before operating, and that was probably the only clean part on his whole body.

"Thanks, son," Jedediah said when he had finished drinking. "I needed that water. I was dyin' of thirst."

"Where are you from, Jed?" Darrell asked. "You have a different accent." There was a twang in Jed's accent that Darrell liked.

"Well, lemme tell y'all a funny story. Ya see, before this here war got started, I was livin' in Virginny. Then my daggum state left the good ole US of A. All of us fellers who lived on the west side of the state got mad at the rich snobs who lived on the east side of the state 'cuz they quit on our country. So we quit on them and formed our own state. I guess now I live in what they call West Virginny. Ain't that a hoot—secedin' from a seceder." Jed laughed like what he said was the funniest joke that he had ever heard. He rolled on the grass in laughter.

"Hey, did you hear the one 'bout the woman from Alabamy?" Jed spoke. He then proceeded to tell Darrell the dirtiest joke that he had ever heard. The punch line was so disgusting that Darrell's face burned with embarrassment. It turned five shades of red. Evidently, that was the reaction that Jedediah had hoped for, because he laughed harder than he had before. Not only was his body filthy, Darrell thought, but his jokes were ten times as dirty.

But there was something about Jed that Darrell liked. He was so filled with life. In a place where many of the soldiers looked like death was knocking at their door, Jedediah was alive and exuberant.

"Jed, that was the most disgusting joke I've ever heard," Darrell said to the soldier.

"I got me a million of 'em. Ya wanna hear another one?" Jed asked when he finally stopped laughing.

"No!" Darrell cried emphatically. "I'm still trying to get rid of the image created by the last one. Here, you want some of these biscuits?"

Jed took a few pieces of hard tack. They were so tough that Darrell didn't know how he would be able to eat it with his four teeth. But Jed took a piece of hard tack and gummed it until his saliva softened it enough for him to swallow it.

"Thank ye kindly, Darrell," Jedediah said. "I can't wait till I get back home and have me some good ole possum stew or a squirrel san'wich. The grub they feed you in this here army ain't no good."

"Well, I guess I have to go to the next soldier now, Jed. You take care of yourself. Captain Robinson said that you're gonna get transported to a barn or a church or someone's house soon," Darrell said. He was so happy that Jed wasn't going to die in front of him, but he wanted to get out of there as soon as he could, just in case Jed took a turn for the worse.

"I hope they don't take me to no church. The good Lord's probably so mad that I ain't been in his house in so long that he'll strike me down before I get inside. Hey, Darrell, before you leave, can you do something for me?"

"Sure Jed. What do you want?"

Jedediah held up his hand and stuck out his dirty index finger. "Give this here finger a pull, will ye?"

Darrell thought that it was a strange request. Then he thought that maybe the finger had been injured somehow, and pulling on it would make it feel better. So he took the finger and pulled. He soon regretted doing it. When he pulled on the finger, Jedediah Washburn let out the loudest, smelliest gas that Darrell had ever experienced. The smell was awful. Darrell grabbed his nose, but the odor still worked its way inside of his nostrils. He worried that his clothes would permanently retain this offensive odor. The cloud of putrid gas spread to where other soldiers were. They cursed at Jedediah and threw rocks or whatever they could find at him. Jed didn't care. He laughed and laughed, even when rocks were pelting him. Darrell shook his head. He had never met a man like Jedediah Washburn before, and he wasn't too sure if he ever wanted to meet another one. It was hard not to laugh at the soldier—but that smell was so awful that he had to go quite a ways away from him before he didn't smell it anymore.

After leaving Jed, Darrell felt more secure about working with the wounded soldiers. He went from one to another, helping each of them. He talked to them about hometowns and learned about faraway places. He saw pictures of wives and girlfriends. Some soldiers worried about their lives and how they were going to function without an arm or a leg, and Darrell listened to their anxieties.

Darrell found that he liked sitting with the soldiers and talking about anything that they wanted to talk about. The soldiers also appreciated someone to talk to. Sometimes he spent too much time with one soldier and had to be prompted by Private Morris to keep moving along.

"Darrell, come over here for a moment," Captain Robinson said.

"Yes, sir," Darrell answered.

"It looks like you're doing better caring for the soldiers. Do you want to learn how to change their bandages?"

"I don't know about that, Captain Robinson," Darrell said nervously. "I don't know if I can take seeing what their wounds look like."

"Let's just give it a try. It would really help me out if you could change the dressings for me. Just unwrap the old bandage carefully, like this." Captain Robinson began unwrapping the bandage from a wounded soldier. "If you do it slow like this it won't cause too much pain for the soldier."

Darrell braced himself to seeing the wound. In his mind, he pictured a bone sticking out from where Captain Robinson had cut the arm or the leg. What he found out was that the wound was already covered with a flap of skin. Captain Robinson told Darrell that when he amputated an arm or a leg, he kept a portion of skin around the wound so that he could wrap it back around the amputated part and stitch the injury closed. He told Darrell that this would prevent infection.

When Darrell first saw the soldier's amputated area, he remembered the time when Terry McIntyre showed him his wound. Terry's injury had already healed, and this soldier's wound still looked like it had a long way to go before it would look better. It had a little blood leaking out of the stitching. The wound wasn't a pretty sight, but still the injury didn't look as bad as Darrell thought it would. Changing bandages wasn't going to be as revolting as he thought.

"Now you take the new bandage and wrap it around the wound. Not too tight, though," Captain Robinson instructed.

Captain Robinson monitored Darrell as he placed the new bandage around the injury. He nodded his approval of Darrell's wrapping. Darrell quickly learned how to expertly wrap the bandages around the wound. Working with the ambulance corps wasn't so bad after all.

When he was finished, Private Morris and Captain Robinson both came over to show their appreciation for how well Darrell had performed his duties. They were proud of him that he had worked through his fears.

"You did a real good job, Darrell," Private Morris told him.

"Thanks, Private Morris. What helped me a lot was that none of the other of the soldiers that I worked on this morning died. That helped me to settle down. I like helping out."

Darrell remembered that earlier in the day he had looked down on Private Morris because he wasn't a fighting soldier. Now he saw him in a new light, and he respected the work that Private Morris did in caring for the wounded. He realized that being a part of the ambulance corps was an important job in the army.

# Chapter 12

## COLONEL CHAMBERLAIN'S DEFENSE

Darrell and Private Jimmy Morris sat down after ministering to the wounded soldiers. Members of the ambulance corps were already loading the injured and taking them to places where they would get more constant care. Many people in Gettysburg and the outlying areas had opened their houses to take care of the wounded soldiers. Churches had also volunteered to help. Darrell wondered who would take care of Jedediah Washburn. He hoped that it would be a barn for the people's sake. His body odor would fit in just right in a barn full of horses.

Private Morris got up and went over to talk to Captain Robinson. When he returned he was ready to get back to work.

"Captain Robinson said you can come along with me today. But you have to listen to me and do everything I say—got it?" Private Morris said sounding very military.

"What do I have to do?" Darrell asked.

"Come on, and follow me," Private Morris said. "You see, we're going to the battlefield. We'll wait for the action to end, and then me and you will get the wounded soldiers back to Captain Robinson and the other doctors so they can operate on 'em."

Private Morris led Darrell to a bunch of wagons parked on the edge of the field where the injured soldiers were lying. There were eight to ten of the wagons parked together. They looked like ordinary wagons with a canvass covering. Inside the wagons were three bed-like structures.

"You see these?" Private Morris pointed to the three portable beds. "These are called stretchers. We put the wounded boys on these and carry them back to the wagon."

"What's all the bandages for?" Darrell asked, seeing a large pile of cloth strips.

"Those are for tying tourniquets. You see when we come upon a soldier who is bleeding pretty bad, we tie the cloth real tight to help stop the bleeding. Then we can get the soldier back to the hospital without them dying on us. Here, lemme show you how to tie one."

Private Morris tied a cloth around Darrell's arm. He didn't tighten it as hard as he would on the battlefield because he didn't want to completely stop the blood flowing through Darrell's arm. Then he quickly untied the bandage.

"When I'm tying it for real, I'll tighten the cloth as hard as I can. The soldier's probably gonna lose the arm or leg anyway, so the most important thing is to stop the bleeding and keep the soldier alive. Now you tie it on me," Private Morris told Darrell, and he supervised Darrell's tourniquet tying technique until Darrell did it correctly.

"Now let's go get Nellie," Private Morris said and began walking to a small makeshift corral that held a bunch of horses. Private Morris went to a big, roan-colored horse that walked over to them when it spotted Jimmy.

"Nellie's my horse. She's as strong as an ox. It don't take her nothing to pull the wagon with three soldiers in it. Here you go, Nellie," and Private Morris gave Nellie an apple to eat. He then took her out of the corral and brought her back to his wagon.

Private Morris hitched Nellie up to the wagon, and then he and Darrell boarded the front seat. "Captain Robinson said that the army expects Lee to attack the left and the right ends of our defensive position today. He's already sent some ambulances to the right side, and he wants me and you to go to the left. He expects some heavy fighting today. Remember—listen to me all the time, and do exactly as I say. I'll be in big trouble if you get shot. Do you hear me?"

"I'll do whatever you want me to do—I promise," Darrell said. He was a part of the army now. He wasn't in the fighting that he had originally come to Gettysburg to be a part of, but he really felt like a member of the ambulance corps. He would treat Private Morris not as a friend but as his commanding officer.

Private Morris drove the wagon into a wooded area. After traveling for some time, he stopped and got down from the wagon.

"We'll keep Nell up here. This way there's no chance that a stray bullet will hit her. We can't afford to lose Nellie. There'd be no way to get the wounded back to the field hospital without her."

After tying Nellie's reins to a tree, Private Morris left her with a little bucket of water. Then he motioned for Darrell to come deeper into the woods. There were sounds of officers ordering soldiers around. This was much closer to the battlefield than Darrell and Kenny had been on the previous day. Darrell's heart started pounding as Private Morris led them closer to where he could see the soldiers.

"We'll stay here," he told Darrell. "We can see the battle, but we should still be safe. When the shooting commences, lie down, and don't ever get back up. Not even if there's a loll in the action. You stay down. You never know when some rebel seeing some kind of movement will fire at you."

"Believe me—my heart's racing so fast that I won't move once the shooting starts," Darrell nervously said to Private Morris.

Private Morris looked at Darrell. He wanted to help calm him down. "We're okay here. I wouldn't get you too close to the action. Just stay down, and you'll be all right."

Private Morris and Darrell looked at the surroundings. The woods were so thick that little sunlight was able to break through. The wooded area was also a little cooler than where the field hospital was because it was out of the sun. It was a welcome relief from the heat and humidity. Ahead of them was a group of soldiers. On a ledge looking over the top of a hill were two officers. One was directing the traffic of the Union army, and the other one was listening to him. When Private Morris spotted the two officers, he became excited.

"Hey, remember when I told about the colonel who was a lawyer from Erie and was gonna help me get into Harvard? Well, that's him down there on the right—the one with the long sideburns. His name is Colonel Vincent—Colonel Strong Vincent. Let's go down and say hi."

Before Darrell could say anything, Private Morris had already made it halfway down the hill to where the officers were standing. Darrell decided to follow him.

"Colonel Vincent, it's me—Private Jimmy Morris. How are you, sir?" He had interrupted whatever Colonel Vincent and the other officer were talking about. Colonel Vincent didn't look upset, and instead of returning Private Morris' salute, he held out his hand in friendship.

"Private Morris, it's good to see you again. Colonel Chamberlain, this is Private Jimmy Morris. Private Morris, this is Colonel Joshua Chamberlain." Private Morris saluted Colonel Chamberlain, who returned his salute.

"Private Morris here is the best member of the ambulance corps that we've got," Colonel Vincent went on. "Now, Jimmy, the fighting's gonna get hot around here. Promise me you'll stay in the area and give our wounded boys the best attention that you can."

"You can count on me, Colonel Vincent," Private Morris said.

"Good man," Colonel Vincent answered, and then continued his discussion with Colonel Chamberlain. "Now, Josh, as I was saying, our defensive position begins far to the right at a place called Culp's Hill. It follows almost a straight line until it gets here. You are the extreme left of our defensive position. Protect yourself from attacks from your front and from your left. Under no circumstances can you retreat—you must hold this position at all costs. You're gonna have to stay and fight to your last man. If the Confederates get this position, then they can chew up our whole defensive line right back to Culp's Hill. This place, Little Round Top, must not be surrendered. If we lose it, we might lose the whole battle of Gettysburg. My forces will be on your right, and we have the same orders—we cannot give up the position. Do you understand the circumstances in which I have placed your army?"

"Yes, I do, Colonel Vincent. My boys will protect this position with all they've got," Colonel Chamberlain responded.

Darrell looked at both officers. They both knew the dire situation that they were in, but both seemed unafraid. Colonel Vincent looked back at Private Morris one last time.

"Remember, Jimmy. These soldiers will need the best care after this fight. Make sure that they get it."

"Yes, sir," Private Morris said, and he began to return to his spot. Darrell stayed for a minute to watch the two colonels depart.

"Good luck to you, Joshua," Colonel Vincent said as he shook Chamberlain's hand.

"And to you too," Colonel Chamberlain responded, and then the two officers went to take care of the alignment of their soldiers.

Darrell raced back to where he and Private Morris would observe the battle. Colonel Vincent's orders were still ringing in his ears. The army could not retreat—even if they were down to one man defending the position. He thought of how the soldiers ran from the field the previous day. These soldiers could not do the same thing. They had been ordered to stay and fight.

Colonel Chamberlain placed his army in the shape of a capital letter *L*. The long side of the letter would protect against Southern attacks from the front. The short bottom leg of the *L* would protect against rebel assaults from the left side.

"Chamberlain's army looks so small," Darrell said to Private Morris. "Do you think that they can hold off the rebs?"

"We got two things working for us," Private Morris answered. "The first is that we're on the top of a hill. It is much easier to defend the top of a hill than it is to climb up the side of it to try to take the position."

"What's the other advantage?" Darrell asked.

"Do you see what our boys are doing?" Darrell looked and saw the soldiers digging and constructing a small wall. "We have a two-foot-high rock wall that runs along our line of defense. This will give our soldiers protection to fire behind. The rebs are going to have to climb up the side of the hill, and they'll be completely out in the open. Firing at them will be much easier for us."

The soldiers had been in place for less than fifteen minutes when the first rebel assault took place. Suddenly a loud yell could be heard from the bottom of the hill. It was one of the scariest things that Darrell had ever heard. It was the famous "rebel yell." Darrell had read about this cry in the *Dubaville Times*. Soldiers said that when they heard it, their hearts missed a beat. Hearing it for the first time, Darrell understood what the soldiers meant. The yell was in itself enough to get Darrell to want to start running in retreat.

Private Morris looked over at Darrell and put his arm around him. "Don't worry about that noise," he said. "We're safe up here. Just stay down."

The Confederate soldiers began coming up the side of the hill. It was an enormous army. Darrell figured they had almost ten times as many men as Chamberlain's little force. *How can our small army defeat their much larger one?* he thought.

The rebels made it halfway up the hill when Chamberlain's army opened fire. The whole first line of the attacking rebel soldiers went down—dead or wounded. Chamberlain's group reloaded. They sent a second deadly volley into the Confederates. The rebels just stood there and took the bullets. When they tried to fire back, many of their bullets sailed over the heads of the Union army. They were too far down the side of the hill to have an effect on Chamberlain's group. The bullets chewed up the ground in front of Darrell and Private Morris.

"We'll have to move back when the fighting dies down," Private Morris told Darrell. "Their army's too far down the hill to shoot accurately at our boys."

Again and again the Union army fired into the Southern one with deadly accuracy. The rebels tried inching their way forward. This just caused more casualties. They were being slaughtered. After a few minutes, the Confederates decided to go back down the hill and regroup. They dragged some of their wounded back down with them.

Darrell got excited. *That was easy*, he thought. Only one or two of Chamberlain's men had been hit, and the Confederate army lost maybe one hundred soldiers in that brief exchange.

"We won!" Darrell cheered, and he jumped up to his feet to congratulate the soldiers.

Some of Chamberlain's men looked back at Darrell with angry sneers.

*Why are they angry?* Darrell thought. *Shouldn't they be happy that they had just won?*

Suddenly Private Morris's arm grabbed the back of Darrell's shirt and threw him to the ground.

"What are you trying to do, get yourself killed?" he screamed at Darrell. "I told you to stay down!"

"We won, didn't we? I was just cheering the army on their victory," Darrell answered, really confused.

"That was just the first attack. There'll be more of 'em," Private Morris said.

As if obeying Private Morris's prediction, the rebel yell was sounded again. The Confederate army raced back up the hill. In this attack, the soldiers got much farther than the last time. Chamberlain's army blasted into the enemy. The rebels fired back. Confederate bullets began scoring hits into Chamberlain's force. Being farther up the hill had allowed them to take better aim at the Union army. They continued to shout and fire into the Union line. Darrell saw Union soldiers get shot. Some fell, dead before hitting the ground. The death of fellow soldiers didn't seem to affect Chamberlain's men. They kept right on firing at the rebels.

The Confederates crept farther up the side of the hill. Each step got them closer to their enemy. But each step was also paid for with more wounded and dead soldiers. Their casualties littered the hill.

Bullets filled the air. Darrell thought that it looked like a swarm of bees after you smashed their beehive. Just as the air would become thick with angry bees, the air at the battlefield was thick with leaden projectiles. Branches of trees were cut off by stray shots. Both armies kept firing into each other. The number of casualties increased.

"How long will they keep shooting at each other?" Darrell asked Private Morris.

"I don't know, but our soldiers are putting up a good fight," Private Morris answered.

The number of Chamberlain's wounded began to grow. He had been badly outnumbered before. This attack saw more and more of his soldiers being taken out of action. How could they afford to lose so many men?

Darrell saw Colonel Chamberlain standing like a rock. He fired his pistol into the avenging army. He also yelled orders to his soldiers. *What a courageous leader he is*, Darrell thought. The colonel wasn't concerned with his own safety. He knew his orders and was willing to fight alongside his troops to carry them out.

After what seemed like forever, but in truth was less than half an hour, the Confederate troops decided that they had had enough for this round of their assault. They retreated down the side of the hill.

Colonel Chamberlain looked after his wounded soldiers. Although there were many, there were a lot more injured and dead rebel soldiers lying on the side of the hill. Reinforcement soldiers strengthened the Union defensive position. The soldiers prepared for another attack that they knew would be coming.

"Now's a good time to move back a little," Private Morris said to Darrell.

"How long do you think the Union army can fight off the attacks from the rebels?" Darrell asked.

Before Private Morris could answer, the now familiar rebel yell announced the next attack. The Confederate army worked its way up the side of the hill. Darrell looked at the faces of Chamberlain's force. The larger enemy army did not frighten them. They had a look of angry determination on their faces.

Darrell looked at the ground that they were protecting. The wooded area that he was clearing back at home was twenty times as large as this small plot of land. But this area was deemed valuable—so valuable that it could not be lost. The soldiers were determined not to give it up. Darrell saw the nobleness of these soldiers.

Again, bullets filled the air. Gun smoke fogged the entire area of fighting. The Confederates inched forward. Darrell thought that if they could take ten big steps forward, they would be at the Union's stone wall. The number of injured increased on both sides. Wounded body fell on wounded body. The Confederates could scarcely walk up the side of the hill without tripping over one of their comrades. Chamberlain's soldiers were also taking a pounding. The rifles never stopped firing. Soldiers never stopped falling.

Darrell kept thinking about what Colonel Vincent had said to Colonel Chamberlain: "You're gonna have to stay and fight to your last man." What if it came down to that—one man alone on the hill trying to fight off a wave of Confederates? If they lost the hill—they might lose the battle of Gettysburg. Wasn't that what Colonel Vincent had said?

Darrell could now see the faces of the rebel soldiers. They had that same angry determination on their faces that Chamberlain's men had. Maybe they had been told to fight to their last man too. It didn't seem to matter how many men they had lost so far. The hill had to be taken. The soldiers were determined to do it. These were two stubborn forces who shot angrily at each other with deadly accuracy.

Once more, after the fighting had gone on for what seemed like forever, the rebel army retreated down the hill.

"Colonel Chamberlain," Darrell heard a soldier say. "We're running out of ammunition."

"Get what you can from the dead and wounded," Colonel Chamberlain answered. "That's all we've got to fight with."

The Union soldiers quickly scavenged around to get whatever bullets they could find. Then they heard the rebel yell again.

"They keep coming. When will they stop attacking?" Darrell asked Private Morris.

"I dunno. The situation is getting pretty bad though," Private Morris said.

The rebels ran up the side of the hill. They were closer than ever to the Union lines. The shooting was almost at point-blank range.

Then the Confederates ran the last few yards to the stone wall and jumped over it. The two armies were locked in hand-to-hand combat. Darrell saw one of Chamberlain's men shoot a rebel who was standing less than a foot from him. The impact of the bullet sent the Southern soldier flying over ten feet. He went over the stone wall and rolled down the hill. Then the same Union soldier turned his gun around. With the butt end of the rifle, he slammed a second rebel right in the stomach. As the soldier bent down from the blow, the Union soldier brought the butt end of the rifle up and smashed the Confederate's jaw. The soldier fell back in pain.

Never in Darrell's wildest thoughts did he imagine that war would be like this. What he saw looked more like two angry mobs than two armies. The soldiers shot each other. They punched each other. They kicked each other. And they beat each other with their rifles. Darrell had come to Gettysburg to join the army. This was something that he didn't think he could ever do. When Terry McIntyre had come home from the war and told his stories of the fighting, he never mentioned anything that was as brutal as this. Darrell used to think war was glorious. Where was the glory in the midst of this punching and beating?

The Confederate army began pushing the Union soldiers back. They still had an advantage in numbers. Colonel Chamberlain had his pistol out. He was firing unceasingly at the rebels. The Confederates looked as if they would sweep away the enemy. Darrell kept wondering if this was finally where the Union soldiers would retreat. Who could blame them? They had fought hard. Now they were being battered by the rebels.

Suddenly, Union reinforcements entered the fray. They fired into the enemy at point-blank range. This helped Chamberlain's men push back. By some miracle, the Confederate army was driven back over the wall and down the hill. This latest assault was finally over.

Darrell could only admire the strength and conviction of the Union army. They would not retreat, and they were going to fight to their last man.

The last Confederate charge had taken a terrible toll on Chamberlain's army. The number of dead and wounded was reaching alarming proportions. Cries went up that ammunition was at a critical shortage. Colonel Chamberlain just stood there, trying to assess what to do next. The rebels would be back, but how was he ever going to hold off another attack with so little ammunition?

Private Morris stood up and turned back to Darrell. "You stay here, you hear? I wanna go talk to Colonel Chamberlain."

Private Morris went down to speak to the officer. Whatever he had to say, Colonel Chamberlain answered with a nod of his head. Private Morris looked over the wounded soldiers, reached down, and grabbed a rifle and ammunition. He then walked back up to Darrell.

"I just can't sit here and watch anymore. If I don't do something, I'll never forgive myself. You stay here. I'm going down to fight with Chamberlain's men."

"But, Private Morris, I wanna be with you," Darrell cried.

"You come down there, and I'll shoot you myself," snapped Private Morris. "Colonel Chamberlain said that the situation is desperate. He's going to order a bayonet charge. You see this thing that looks like a knife? This is a bayonet. It goes on the front of the rifle. When the rebs start coming up the hill, Colonel Chamberlain's going to order us to run right into them. It's gotta work. Remember what Colonel Vincent said would happen if we lost Little Round Top?"

"He said we might also lose the battle of Gettysburg. But, Jimmy, you can't go. What if you get shot? What am I supposed to do then?" He called him Jimmy instead of Private Morris because he had genuine concern for his safety. Jimmy was his friend.

"Darrell, it's time for you to grow up. If something happens to me, when the battle is over, go and get Nellie. Bring her down here and start working on the soldiers. You know how to tie a tourniquet. I taught you myself."

"What do I do then?" Darrell asked.

"Go get a soldier to help you lift the wounded into the wagon. Get the wounded back to Captain Robinson as fast as you can. When you get there, tell him that something has happened to me, and he'll assign a new soldier to work with you."

"But, Jimmy, I don't know if I can do everything by myself," Darrell said nervously.

"Sure you can. Remember, those boys are all heroes down there. How they've been able to hold off them rebels, I don't know. But they deserve the best doctoring you can give 'em. But not by a boy—they need a man to help them. So quit your crying."

"But, Jimmy, I'm scared," Darrell said.

"I'm scared, too. Colonel Chamberlain's taking a big gamble, but what else is there to do? He's got no ammunition, and he's lost a lot of soldiers. We're either gonna win this fight on this charge, or we're gonna lose it. Either way, it's his best option. You stay strong. Think of the wounded boys who need you. Can you do that?"

"I'll try," Darrell answered as he tried to regain his composure.

"Darrell, are you a Christian? Do you believe in God?" Private Morris asked.

"Yes."

"Then pray as hard as you can that this attack works. Pray as you've never prayed before. If God is willing, then I'll see you soon."

With that, Private Morris went back down and took a place in Chamberlain's line.

Suddenly, Darrell heard Colonel Chamberlain yell, "Fix bayonets!"

His whole army grabbed their bayonets and at once complied with the order. An angry growl went up along Chamberlain's line.

The rebel yell could be heard from down the hill. The rebels were coming again.

Colonel Chamberlain waited and then screamed out, "Okay, men! *Charge!*"

Now a louder growl was yelled by his troops. Then his tiny force jumped over the wall and ran down the hill into the teeth of the Confederate army.

# Chapter 13

## CHAMBERLAIN'S CHARGE

After the soldiers left the defensive position that they had fought so hard to guard all day, Darrell closed his eyes. He began to pray harder than he had ever prayed before. He pleaded with God to let the Union army win. Darrell was afraid to open his eyes for fear that he would see the Confederates swarming up the hill. He prayed again for victory. Then he got an idea. He decided to bargain with God to try to help win the battle.

"Please, God . . . please let Chamberlain's men win! I promise I won't cause my mom and dad any more problems. I'll even learn to like Jeremiah! I'll never beat on him again. I promise. Please let them win. And please keep Jimmy Morris alive. Please, God . . . I'm begging you!"

When Darrell opened his eyes, he saw a Confederate soldier walking up to the top of the hill. Immediately he closed his eyes again.

*They lost? Please, God, tell me that they didn't lose.* What would he do if they lost? Would the rebels let him take the wounded back to Captain Robinson? Darrell closed his eyes tighter than before. Could God change the result of the battle after it had been decided?

When he opened his eyes again, he saw the same Confederate soldier, but behind him was one of Chamberlain's men aiming his rifle at the rebel's back. The Confederate was a prisoner of war! Chamberlain's men hadn't lost at all. Darrell saw more Confederate soldiers, each one with a Union soldier behind him. It was true.

Chamberlain's little army had defeated the much larger Confederate force!

Darrell lost all control and began jumping up and down, yelling and screaming his congratulations. The first time he did this, it was met with angry looks from Chamberlain's men. Now as they looked up to see the cheering boy, smiles appeared on their faces, and they nodded their heads in appreciation of Darrell's praise.

Darrell was elated. He had run away from home to see General Lee's forces get beat by the Union army. It wasn't the whipping that he had hoped to see. But it was a great victory nonetheless. Colonel Chamberlain's men had barely hung on to win the day. The Confederate prisoners of war were being marched up the hill.

But what about Private Morris? Darrell searched the soldiers, trying to find him. At first, it seemed he was not there. Suddenly, he came marching up the hill, a Confederate prisoner of war in front of him. Private Morris had the biggest smile on his face. He gave his prisoner to another soldier and ran up to meet Darrell. Darrell ran down the hill. When he came up to Private Morris, he stopped, stood straight, and saluted him. Private Morris smiled and returned the salute. Then the two embraced.

"You shoulda seen it, Darrell!" Private Morris said. "We went right down into the rebs. They looked so shocked to see us charging into them. Some of them shot at us and then turned and ran. Some stood there frozen and threw down their weapons. Most of them just turned and ran. I bet you that they're still running. They probably won't stop until they're outta Pennsylvania. Colonel Chamberlain's charge worked. It really worked! He's a genius! I'm gonna keep this rifle as a remembrance of what went on here today!"

"I'm so glad you're alive," Darrell told him.

"C'mon. Let's get Nellie and get these brave boys back to the field hospital."

"No, Private Morris. I'll get Nellie and the ambulance. You stay here and be with the other victorious soldiers!" Darrell exclaimed, and ran off to get Nellie.

When Darrell returned with the ambulance, Private Morris was talking with some of the prisoners of war. He had given one of them his canteen so that he could get a drink. Other Northern soldiers were doing the same—talking casually with the rebel prisoners. Darrell thought it was strange to be mortal enemies one minute and sharing a drink of water and conversation the next. He didn't think he would ever understand war.

Private Morris saw Darrell and moved to a wounded soldier. Darrell ran over to him with bandages and a stretcher.

"That was some battle," Darrell said to the soldier, whose left arm was injured. "I've never seen anything like it. I swear you guys have to be the bravest soldiers ever."

"Thank you, son," the soldier said to Darrell.

"I'm Darrell Stouffer. I'm honored to be helping you."

"My name's Mark Taylor," the soldier exclaimed. He could only smile at Darrell's hero-worship of the soldiers. When Private Taylor spoke, he had a different accent. Instead of saying Mark Taylor, it sounded more like *Mahk Taylah*.

"Gee that's a great accent," Darrell went on. "Where are you boys from?"

"We're Maine men. This here is the Twentieth Maine. You would be good to remember that."

"I'll never forget it or the fight you put up today," Darrell said.

As he talked to Private Taylor, Private Morris tied the tourniquet. When he was done, Private Taylor walked over to the ambulance to be transported. It was good to have Darrell there to make conversation with the soldiers. That allowed Private Morris to work on the wounded soldiers without interruptions. The injured soldiers didn't seem to even notice that he was ministering to their wounds.

Private Morris and Darrell worked on two other soldiers, and then they helped Private Taylor and those men into the ambulance. Nellie seemed to know the urgency of her trip because she quickly pulled the ambulance back to the field hospital. Private Morris was right when he had said that Nellie was as strong as an ox because the weight in the back of the ambulance didn't seem to bother her at all.

"You wanna hear the story of the charge again, Darrell?" Private Morris said excitedly on their way to the field hospital.

"Yeah, go ahead," Darrell said, and Private Morris told him the story again.

When they reached the field hospital, the surgeons had already begun their work on wounded soldiers from other parts of the battlefield. Darrell wanted to find Captain Robinson and tell him about the fighting that he had seen. When he did find him, Captain Robinson was in the middle of surgery. He had a saw that he was using to cut through a soldier's leg. Darrell became woozy at the sight of the amputation. Private Morris came over to Darrell.

"It's best not to watch if you're skittish," he said. "I've seen grown men faint watching those guys cutting off arms and legs."

Darrell and Private Morris hurried back to the wounded soldiers of the Twentieth Maine. By the time that they had gotten back to Little Round Top, other ambulances had arrived and their crews were helping wounded soldiers. Private Morris was still in high spirits, and he recited the story of the charge another time for Darrell. Darrell thought he was the happiest person he had ever met.

Private Morris and Darrell began working on a soldier whose leg wound was pretty serious. He was losing a lot of blood. Darrell ran to get a stretcher while Private Morris began tying a tourniquet. As he was working, Colonel Chamberlain came over.

"Hang in there, Johnson," Chamberlain said to the wounded soldier. "Private Morris here will get you back to the doctors right away."

"Colonel Chamberlain, could I have a word with you?" a general said as he walked over to where Chamberlain was standing.

Colonel Chamberlain saluted the general. "Yes, sir," he answered.

"I wanted to congratulate you, Colonel Chamberlain," the general exclaimed. "That was one heck of a charge. You should be proud of yourself and your soldiers on the fight you put up today."

"Thank you, General," Colonel Chamberlain said. "Can I ask, how did the forces on my right make out?"

"About the same as you. The rebels kept attacking, but our boys fought hard today, and in the end, they held their ground."

"I must go and congratulate Colonel Vincent. If it wasn't for him, we would've never won today. He took responsibility for placing all of the soldiers on Little Round Top. If we would've waited for a general's orders, the rebels would've already taken this ground before we got to it. Colonel Vincent really deserves all of the credit for today's victory."

"I'm sorry to have to tell you this, Colonel Chamberlain, but Colonel Vincent was shot in action today. He's still alive, but the doctors think that his wound is fatal. It's too bad. He was shot leading his men in battle. Well, anyway, good work today, Colonel. I'll put in my report that I think that you deserve a promotion. We need more fighting men like you."

Darrell came running over with a stretcher. Private Morris had suddenly stopped working on the soldier when he heard the general say that Colonel Vincent had been shot.

"What's the matter?" Darrell asked.

"Colonel Vincent's been wounded. The general said that he probably won't make it."

"I'm sorry," Darrell said, trying to console Private Morris.

Darrell looked at Private Morris. He saw the remorse in his face. Private Morris wasn't upset because the person who was going to get him into Harvard was dying. He was upset that someone who he liked and cared about had been mortally wounded.

The rest of the day, Private Morris worked in silence. No more smiling, no more retelling the story of Chamberlain's charge—just working on the wounded. Darrell did all of the talking with the wounded soldiers, making them feel better through their little conversations.

As the sun began to go down, Darrell started walking back to the McElroy house. He had a lot of stories to tell Uncle Levi and Aunt Clara. He had seen General Lee's men lose in battle. It took a superhuman effort, but the North had beaten the South. This was the moment that he had hoped he would see—the Confederates getting beat by the Union army. It was one of the main reasons that he had run away from home and was why he did not leave earlier that morning with Kenny. He had also taken care of the brave soldiers who made that victory happen.

Darrell sneaked back through the Union lines and through the town of Gettysburg until he reached the McElroy residence. He was tired and hungry and full of wondrous tales to tell.

# Chapter 14

# THE KISS

When Darrell went inside the McElroy residence, Uncle Levi and Aunt Clara greeted him. They did not look happy.

"What happened to Kenny, now?" Aunt Clara exclaimed.

"He's okay," Darrell said. "This morning he decided to go back home. He had had enough of the war, and he wanted to go back to farming."

"You just let him go home alone where he'd have to walk past the entire Confederate army?" Aunt Clara scowled.

"Kenny'll be okay. He can scoot around them rebs easy enough. I wasn't worried about him. He also promised that he'd stop by my house to let my family know that I'm okay."

"I think he'll be okay, Clara," Uncle Levi said. "Relax—I think Darrell's right. Kenny can make it home without getting caught. And even if the rebs do stop him, what are they going to do with a kid? I'm sure that they'd just let him keep on going—especially because he was heading away from the fighting, not toward it."

"Mr. and Mrs. McElroy, can I ask you a favor?" Darrell asked nervously. "With Kenny gone, I don't have a place to stay. I'm not related to all of you, but I'd sure appreciate it if you'd let me stick around here for a few days."

"Sure, Darrell," Uncle Levi said. "Our door is always open to you—especially after you risked your life to come and get me yesterday."

"Thank you, sir," Darrell said. "I don't know what I'd do if you said no. I'm really tired after today's fighting. I could use a place to get a good night's sleep. I have some great stories to tell you about what happened today."

Darrell then told the family about what he had done all day. He described how he found the pile of body parts, made friends with members of the ambulance crew, helped the wounded, and watched the battle for Little Round Top. Uncle Levi, Aunt Clara, and Elizabeth were captivated by Darrell's stories. They had heard the guns and cannons being fired all day, but they did not know how the battle was going.

"I'm happy that you didn't fight in the battle," Uncle Levi said. "Everyone here was worried that you and Kenny were taking part in the fighting. We were worried that something bad might have happened. I'm glad to see that you're okay. And I'm happy that you were helping the wounded soldiers. I've fought in a war before, and I know how important the medical corps is."

"We had some excitement around here, too. Right, Levi?" Aunt Clara said.

"Yeah, two Confederate soldiers crashed into the house this morning looking for any Union soldiers who might be hiding here," Uncle Levi answered. "A bunch of townspeople had taken in injured Union soldiers after yesterday's battle, and the rebs were making sure that we weren't hiding any injured soldiers.

"That must've been scary," Darrell said. "Did they destroy anything in the house looking for soldiers?"

"No, but when they didn't find any of them, they looked around for food," Uncle Levi replied. "They took everything they could find. The only things that they left behind were the fruits and vegetables that you picked and hid yesterday. We don't have much left to eat, but at least we have something."

"Tell him about how you almost got your head blown off," Aunt Clara said.

"When the fighting started," Uncle Levi said, "I ran outside to see what was happening. A bunch of rebels yelled at me—told me to take cover in the basement. The girls went downstairs, but I tried to see what was going on through the upstairs window."

"That's when we almost lost Levi here," Aunt Clara butted in.

"Yeah, a bullet went right through the window I was looking out of and almost hit me in the head. I dunno if the soldier who fired it was one of ours or one of the enemy's."

"I kept yelling for Levi to come down into the basement," Aunt Clara said, "but he just had to see the fighting for himself."

"I told you I was all right," Uncle Levi said. Then he turned back to Darrell to finish his story. "I found some old wood lying around and boarded up the windows in the front of the house for protection. She won't have to worry about me getting shot anymore," he said, nodding to his wife.

Darrell laughed at how Aunt Clara and Uncle Levi bantered at the table. At home, his mother ruled the household, and his father barely said two words.

"So, Darrell, I'm glad to hear that we fared better in the fighting today than we did yesterday," Uncle Levi said.

"We beat the rebs," Darrell said. "It took quite an effort to do it, though. I've never seen people more determined than the soldiers who fought at Little Round Top today."

It had been a long day, and Darrell was tired. Everyone sat down for a small dinner composed of the little bit of food that was left in the house. Darrell thought of how great the dinner was the night before. Aunt Clara had served potatoes and roast and fresh vegetables to go along with freshly baked bread and cookies. On this night, however, there were peas and beans and strawberries, and not a whole lot more. The Confederates had taken the rest away.

Darrell stumbled his way wearily up to his room. He fell into bed without removing any of his clothes. A few minutes later, there was a soft tap on the door. Elizabeth walked in to talk, just as she had done the previous evening. Even though he was really tired, Darrell thought Elizabeth was a welcome sight.

"I wish you would've been here this morning when the rebels came into the house," Elizabeth said. "I was so scared. They looked so mean."

"Yeah," Darrell answered. "But your dad was here to protect you. I saw some pretty mean-looking rebels myself today. They just kept attacking and attacking the Union lines. I still can't believe that Chamberlain's small army actually beat them."

"I miss Kenny. Do you think he'll be all right walking back home by himself?" Elizabeth asked.

"He's probably already made it back home by now. I probably shouldn't have dragged him along with me in the first place. I was so scared for him yesterday. He looked so awful when he froze up after watching that soldier die. I thought I did something permanent to him. I was so relieved when he snapped out of it."

"Sometimes I wish I could've gone with him to Dubaville," Elizabeth said. "Then I'd be safe away from the battle and those mean-looking rebels."

"You'll be safe here with your parents," Darrell explained. "All you have to remember is not to take any chances."

"But you do," Elizabeth uttered, with a sense of admiration of Darrell. "I don't think you're afraid of anything. I wish I had your courage."

"I was mighty scared today, Elizabeth," Darrell said. "Private Morris left me alone when he charged down the hill into the rebels, and I was really scared. I'm just so grateful that he made it back all right. I think that it's okay to be scared. There's nothing to be ashamed of in being frightened."

"Thanks. Well, I better let you get some sleep," Elizabeth said compassionately. "You look so tired."

Just then, Darrell remembered what Kenny had told him that morning. He had said that Elizabeth told him that she really liked him. He had almost forgotten about this. Even though Darrell felt the same about Elizabeth, it was hard to tell her his feelings. It was easier to tease her about what Kenny had said.

"So, Elizabeth," Darrell smugly said. "I was talking to Kenny this morning, and he said that you told him something about me yesterday."

Elizabeth spun around with a look of horror on her face. Darrell saw this, and he knew he had her. This was going to be fun to make her squirm a little.

"Wha—what did he say?" Elizabeth asked.

"Well, let me try to remember," Darrell said.

"C'mon, Darrell, please tell me," Elizabeth said. She knew that Kenny had revealed her feelings to Darrell.

"Well . . . I think . . . he said something like . . . that you told him that you thought that I was good looking. What did you tell him? Um, you like me a lot?"

Elizabeth's face turned red with embarrassment. Darrell knew that he was in charge now. *This is so easy*, he thought.

"That Kenny. Wait till he comes back here. I'll get even with him for sure," Elizabeth said angrily. Then she asked, "So how do you feel about me?"

"I dunno. Lemme see. How do I feel about you? Hmm," he said, pretending to be deep in thought. He was laughing inside to himself. Expressing his feelings to a girl was hard for Darrell, but teasing came naturally to him.

Then he looked at Elizabeth. Her face was torn with uncertainty. Darrell wasn't sure if she was going to start crying. He felt so bad that he was responsible for making her feel this way. He was having fun teasing her, but now he regretted playing around with her feelings. Why should he harass Elizabeth like this? He liked her; what was wrong with coming right out and admitting it?

"I'm sorry, Elizabeth. I didn't mean to make you feel bad. I was just teasing," Darrell comforted. "The truth is that the moment I saw you, I thought that you were the prettiest girl I'd ever seen. I really like you, Elizabeth. I never said that to a girl before—probably cuz I never felt this way before."

Now Elizabeth's face was turning red again, but it was from embarrassment at Darrell's kind words.

"That is the nicest thing a boy has ever said to me. Thank you, Darrell."

"When Kenny said that he wanted to go back home, I worried that I would never see you again," Darrell said. "I'm sure glad that your father said that I could still stay here."

"So am I," Elizabeth said. "Maybe I should go now. You probably want to get some sleep."

"Wait, Elizabeth. I'll walk you to the door." Darrell got to his feet and walked up close to Elizabeth. The two looked at each other without saying a word. Darrell reached down and took Elizabeth's hand. Her skin was soft. The two stopped at the bedroom door and turned to each other.

Darrell wanted to kiss her goodnight, but he had never kissed a girl before. What if he goofed it up? She'd laugh at him. His heart was pounding so hard that he thought it would burst right out of his body. Elizabeth stood by the door looking at him. There was an uneasy silence. Darrell thought that Elizabeth was probably waiting for him to do something, but he had suddenly become frozen stiff.

Darrell decided to just kiss her and hope for the best. He closed his eyes and moved toward Elizabeth. Lips touched lips. As soon as Darrell's lips came in contact with Elizabeth's, a charge of electricity surged through his body, and he pulled back. He didn't kiss her for long—maybe a tenth of a second. It was just a brief caress of lips, but it was the greatest moment of Darrell's life.

He looked at Elizabeth, and she was smiling so brightly that he could feel the warmth of her expression. He had done that—he had made her feel so good that she communicated it to him through her smile. This was such a great feeling. He felt bad that he had teased Elizabeth earlier instead of coming out with his true feelings for her right away.

Elizabeth turned and fumbled with the doorknob, trying to get out of the room. When she finally opened the door, she turned around one last time to look at Darrell. She flashed him that smile again. Darrell's heart pounded with delight. Then Elizabeth silently closed the door, and Darrell was left with the memory of what she looked like as she left the room.

He gently touched his lips. Thoughts of Elizabeth filled his head. He was so tired, but it would be hours until sleep would finally come. Images of Elizabeth would be working on his brain for a long time—images that would interrupt his sleep.

# Chapter 15

## DARRELL'S DISAPPOINTMENTS

Darrell awoke before everyone else in the house. He looked over at the empty bed where Kenny had slept the previous night. He wondered if Kenny had made it home all right. He also wondered if Kenny was in all kinds of trouble for running away with him. Poor Kenny, he was always getting punished for Darrell's big ideas. Kenny never complained, though. The next time he thought of a new prank, Kenny would be right there to help him. He hoped Kenny had stopped by his house to tell his parents that he was okay. Darrell wondered what kind of trouble he would be in once he got home.

Darrell thought about the battle that he had witnessed the previous day. He had gotten to see what he had been hoping to witness—General Lee losing. He figured that Lee would be heading back down South at some point that day.

Darrell decided to help the wounded soldiers just as he did the previous morning. He got dressed as quietly as possible, and then he hurried down the stairs. Because Aunt Clara and Elizabeth didn't get a chance to bake yesterday, there was nothing to eat for a quick breakfast. Darrell thought that Private Morris could probably help him dig up something to eat once he got back to the wounded soldiers' area.

He was surprised to see the Confederate troops were still in town as he sneaked through the streets. He thought that maybe they would retreat to Virginia later in the day.

Once he arrived by Captain Robinson's tent, he took a look at the field of wounded soldiers. There were so many of them—many more than there had been on Thursday morning. Darrell looked around to try to find Private Morris. He checked every place that he could think of, but he was not around. He decided to take the canteens to the creek by himself and fill them with water. He figured that by the time he got back, Private Morris would be there. He found the tent where the canteens were stored and started carrying them off to fill them up for the wounded soldiers.

The morning was hot—hotter than the previous days. The humidity was unbearable, even at this early hour. Breathing was hard, especially when doing work. Darrell was soaked with sweat as he walked down to the creek. He filled all of the canteens and got a good, long drink for himself. The canteens were heavy; he did not have Private Morris to help him carry them back to where the wounded soldiers were lying.

When he finally made it back to the field hospital, Private Morris was still nowhere to be found. Darrell had much more confidence in himself than he had the previous day. He didn't need anyone to tell him how to take care of the wounded soldiers.

Darrell grabbed some hard tack crackers and some of the canteens and started off to help the wounded soldiers. He was happy to see the soldiers that he had brought to the surgeons the night before, especially the ones from the Twentieth Maine.

"Hey, Darrell!" Private Taylor yelled to him. "Bring that water over here. We're all thirsty."

There were eight soldiers from the Twentieth Maine that had gathered together. Darrell went over to help them, but he also wanted to talk with them.

"How are you guys doing this morning?" Darrell asked.

"Better after we get some water. It sure is hot today," Private Taylor answered.

"I still can't get over how brave you all were yesterday," Darrell said. "If I had been down there fighting with you, I don't know if I could've stayed and fought like you did. Weren't you scared?"

"You wanna know fear?" another Maine soldier said. "Try navigating a fishing boat through a hurricane. Hey, Mickey, remember the big storm of '59?"

"Yeah. I remember you hiding down inside the boat instead of being on deck with the rest of us," Mickey joked, and the other soldier threw a rock at him in response.

"You fishing guys are always bragging about how tough you are," a soldier named Private Coolidge said. "Try going up into the mountains during a Maine winter and cutting down trees. That's worse than being on any sissy boat."

The soldiers laughed and took turns trying to prove who was more fearless. As Darrell changed their bandages, the Maine soldiers tried to decide whose wound looked the ugliest. Darrell was in his glory, running around among them, talking, and laughing. He was enjoying his work.

"It's a good thing we had soldiers as tough as you on Little Round Top," Darrell said to the group. "You all don't seem to be afraid of anything."

Darrell wanted to stay longer and talk with the Maine men, but he knew there were plenty of other soldiers to attend to. He next met some of the soldiers from the Eighty-Third Pennsylvania. They had fought next to the Maine men. Their battle was just as brutal as Chamberlain's fight.

"There were a lot of times that I thought the rebs would run us over," Corporal Davidson of the Eighty-Third Pennsylvania said to Darrell. "Colonel Vincent helped steady us, though."

"Yeah, until he got shot," Private Fletcher said as Darrell was changing his bandage. "Remember what he was doing when he got hit?"

"Our line was wavering a little," Corporal Davidson said to Darrell, "and then ole Vincent jumped up on a rock and yelled something to us. He was really brave."

"He yelled, 'Don't give an inch!'" Private Fletcher said. "Then down he went—hit by a bullet. But he helped us stay on that hill yesterday. I'm gonna miss Colonel Vincent."

Darrell moved from soldier to soldier confidently. He felt good that he was able to help the wounded soldiers. He came upon a soldier from a Michigan regiment who was lying silently on his back. His left leg had been amputated halfway up his thigh. There wasn't much of the left leg that remained after the amputation.

"Hi, soldier, how about a drink of water?" Darrell offered as he came up to the soldier.

There was no response from him. Darrell thought that maybe the soldier hadn't heard him, and so he repeated his offer a little louder.

"Do you want some water?" The soldier still didn't react to him. "Are you hungry? Do you want something to eat?" Darrell suggested. The soldier just lay on his back silently. "Here, lemme change your bandage." Finally the soldier stirred.

"Leave it alone," he growled.

"I just wanna make sure that you don't get an infection by putting on a clean bandage. I promise that it won't hurt much," Darrell insisted.

"I said, leave it alone! Are you deaf?" the soldier yelled.

"What's the matter? I'm here to help you. I can't help if I don't know what's wrong," Darrell said with concern.

"You know what they do to a horse when it has a bad leg?"

*That was a strange question*, Darrell thought. At least the soldier was talking, and so Darrell decided to answer him.

"Most people put it out of its misery and shoot it. I remember a couple of years ago, my dad had to shoot our plow horse, Whitey, when she fell into a hole and broke one of her front legs," Darrell replied.

"Then why do doctors think they're doing me a favor by keeping me alive and cutting off my leg? Why not put me outta my misery and let me die? Stinking doctors. They don't gotta live the rest of their lives crippled. Look at me!"

"But you're a hero. I was there yesterday at the battlefield. I watched the fighting. All of you soldiers here in this field should get medals for your bravery!" Darrell exclaimed.

"And then what? What do I do when I get home? I'm a farmer for goodness sake. How do I work my farm and feed my family on one leg?"

"Back home in Dubaville, we have a soldier. His name is Terry McIntyre. He came home from the war with one leg. He had a hard time with it for a while. Now he's working at the general store and telling war stories all of the time. It just took a little time for him to get used to his new life."

"But I ain't no store worker—I'm a farmer. My farm's been in my family for over a hundred years. I can't give it up."

Darrell looked at the soldier. He was older than a lot of the soldiers who were injured. He looked like he was even older than his own father. Then an idea came to him.

"Do you have any kids, sir?" Darrell asked.

"Yeah, four boys and a girl. My oldest boy, Willie, is fifteen years old. I got another boy, Seth, that's thirteen. The other ones are much younger."

"Well I'm thirteen, and I have a brother, Jacob, who is twelve. If something ever happened to my father, I'm sure me and my brother could take over and run the farm. I bet your kids could do the same thing. And you never know what you're gonna be able to do once the amputated leg heals. I'm sure that you can still help run the farm doing something. You just gotta get used to your new life and find out what you can and can't do."

The soldier was quiet for a few minutes, taking in what Darrell had suggested. Then he looked down at his amputated leg and complained, "What about my wife? Look at me. How is she gonna love a one-legged thing like me?"

"You gotta quit talking like this. You're a hero, just like all of the other soldiers here. My friend Terry McIntyre's wife stayed by him when he came home. I remember he once told me that they were a lot closer after he came back from the war."

"You think she'll be okay with me coming home crippled?" the soldier asked Darrell.

"I'll bet she'll be happy, because you came home alive. Do you know how many wives will find out in the next few days that their husbands won't be coming home? It's gonna be all right. You just have to give it some time," Darrell comforted.

The soldier was silent for a little while again. Then he turned to Darrell and said, "Thanks, kid. You helped me—you really did. I guess I'll have some of that water you got now."

Darrell was happy to have picked up the soldier's spirits. Some of the Twentieth Maine boys were nearby, and Darrell walked over to ask them to talk with the soldier. When he looked back after a few minutes, all of the soldiers, even the one from Michigan that he had helped, were laughing and talking together.

"Hey, Darrell, come here!" a voice called. When Darrell turned around, he saw that Captain Robinson was the person calling him. Darrell dropped everything and ran over to the officer.

"Yes, sir!" He shouted like the other soldiers and saluted Captain Robinson.

"Relax. Come with me for a few minutes. I want to talk to you," Captain Robinson calmly said as he put his hand on Darrell's shoulder.

"I have something that I want to give to you."

Captain Robinson put his hand in his pocket and took out a patch. It was made of white cloth and was oval. He gave the patch to Darrell.

"Gee, thanks, Captain Robinson. What is this design?"

Darrell ran his finger over the design in the middle of the white patch. It was a long, gold-colored pole. At the top of the pole were two golden wings. Curled around the pole were two snakes.

"This is what is called a caduceus. It's a symbol for medicine, passed down from the ancient Greeks. I want you to have it. Now you're one of the medical team."

"Thanks a lot, Captain Robinson. I'll never lose it."

"I have something else to talk to you about. I've been watching you the past couple of days. You've done some good work here."

"Thank you, sir," Darrell said proudly.

"Did you ever think about becoming a doctor? I think you would make a darn good one," Captain Robinson suggested.

Darrell was taken aback. He was flattered by Captain Robinson's offer. "What do you have to do to become a doctor?"

"You have to go to medical school in college," Captain Robinson answered.

"Excuse me, sir," Darrell said. "I come from a farming family. We ain't poor by any stretch of the imagination, but we also don't have lots of extra money for sending me to college. Thank you, though, for thinking so highly of me."

"Darrell, remember yesterday when I told you that I came from a rich family back in Philadelphia?"

"Yes, sir."

"Well, it wouldn't take anything for me to pay your way through medical school. I just wanna see good people like yourself enter into my profession."

"You would really pay for me to go to college?" Darrell asked.

"Sure. You're young now, and I'm caught up in this war, but it won't last forever. When you're old enough to go to college, hopefully the war will be over, and I'll send for you to come to Philadelphia. There are lots of fine colleges there. I can help you to get into a good one. You can even stay with me and my wife, Theresa."

Darrell's head was swimming. He had thought for years about what he wanted to be when he grew up. Farming was okay, but he had always thought he would do something different. What it was, he did not know.

Now he knew what he wanted to be. He could go to college and become a doctor. He liked helping the wounded soldiers. Now he could make a career out of helping people.

"Captain Robinson, I don't know what to say. I would love to go to college to become a doctor."

He could see himself in a white coat, like Doc Winston wore in Dubaville. Maybe he would take over for him some day. Doc Winston was over seventy years old, and he was always sicker than most of his patients. "Let's go see Doc Stouffer," people would say when they got sick. He could make house calls to the McElroy residence and take care of Kenny and Maggie's children. He was so excited with this news.

"There's one thing that you got to do for me, Darrell," Captain Robinson said, bringing Darrell out of his daydream.

"Anything, Captain Robinson," Darrell said. "You just name it."

"Promise me you'll stay in school. I know farmer's boys like you tend to drop out at your age to help run the farm, but you have to keep going to school."

"Why? You said I was too young for college."

"To get into a good college, you have to pass an entrance examination," Captain Robinson said. "You'll never know enough to pass the test if you drop out of school now. If you can't pass the test, there's nothing that I can do to help you get into college. Promise me that you'll stick it out in school until I call for you to come to Philadelphia. We'll talk more about this later. Right now I'm needed in the field hospital." With that, Captain Robinson walked away, leaving a distraught Darrell Stouffer.

In his mind, Darrell kept picturing the same scene over and over. They were all sitting around the table—Mr. and Mrs. Garber, his mother and father, and himself. He kept hearing Mrs. Garber say, "If you try to come back to school in the fall, you will not be welcome." He would not be welcome to go back to the Dubaville school! He could never keep Captain Robinson's promise. He could never pass the entrance examination. This meant he could never go to college and never be a doctor. How could this happen to him? Just when life was at its highest point, and he had finally found out what he really wanted to be in life, the carpet was pulled out from under him.

Then Darrell saw another vision. His mother was kneeling in the garden. Darrell had just confessed about his latest practical joke with the snakes. His mother said to him, "One day, Darrell Anthony Stouffer, you're gonna regret all the things that you did to Mrs. Garber." Now both scenes kept playing over and over in his head. Why should he have to lose everything just because some grown-ups couldn't take a joke?

Darrell thought harder, and he knew that his mother was right. He should have listened to her and quit playing jokes in school. But how could he have known that he would need school later in life? He was so stupid. He wished it was possible to go back in time and take back all of the silly pranks that he had ever played—but that was impossible. He wished that there was a way out of this situation so that he could still become a doctor.

"Hey, Darrell," a voice called out from behind him, shaking him from his thoughts. He turned around to see Private Morris. "What's the matter—you look like someone just stole your favorite Christmas present or something."

"Aw, forget it," Darrell said. He'd have to think about what to do about school later. "Hey, where were you this morning? I looked for you everywhere."

"I went to find out where they took Colonel Vincent," Private Morris answered. "I found him in a field hospital a mile or so from here."

"How's he doing?" Darrell asked, glad to be thinking of something other than doctors and education.

"The surgeon doesn't think he'll last too much longer. They sent a telegram to his folks in Erie, Pennsylvania. Some of them are racing to get down here before he dies, but they may not make it. His wife couldn't come, though. She's about ready to deliver their first child. It's kinda sad that Colonel Vincent'll never get a chance to see his baby."

"I talked to some of the wounded soldiers from his outfit. They all spoke very highly of him," Darrell said, trying to bolster Private Morris's spirits.

"Yeah, one of the officers standing around Colonel Vincent's tent told me that they're gonna make him a general."

Darrell thought that it was strange to promote a man whom they knew was going to die.

"Anyway, I just saw Captain Robinson. He said that the fighting today will probably come from the middle of our defensive position. He wants me and you to take an ambulance over to that area."

"Wait a minute," Darrell interrupted. "I thought that we won yesterday. Don't you remember the charge down the hill? You said the rebels ran in retreat!"

"Sometimes battles go on for a few days. This one ain't over, yet," Private Morris explained.

"But, I don't get it. They retreated and surrendered yesterday."

"Darrell, let me ask you a question. When you came out here from town, were the rebs still there?"

"Yeah."

"Well then, this ain't over yet. When General Lee pulls his army outta Gettysburg, then you'll know that the battle is over."

Darrell kicked the dirt in disgust. He thought, *First I lost my chance to be a doctor. Now I might lose my chance to see General Lee and the Confederates get beaten because they have another day to fight the Union army.*

"You know something, Private Morris," Darrell said. "Sometimes life just isn't fair."

# Chapter 16

# THE CONFEDERATE BOMBARDMENT

Darrell and Private Morris loaded up the ambulance and began to head to a point that Private Morris called Cemetery Ridge.

"Do you think the fighting will be as bad as yesterday?" Darrell asked.

"I don't know. I hope that we can win the battle today, though," Private Morris said. "Tomorrow is the Fourth of July, and I hope we aren't still fighting when we should be remembering our independence."

Private Morris took the ambulance to where the two of them could see the Union soldiers' position. There was a large concentration of troops that ran along the side of a hill. The Union soldiers had built a stone wall a couple of feet high across their defensive position. The soldiers were just lounging around. Private Morris took the ambulance to a place that was far behind where the Union army was located.

"I think this is a good spot to put Nellie," he said. "She'll be out of range back here, and there's a little bit of shade in this small clump of trees. I'm hungry, Darrell. You wanna try to find something to eat?"

Darrell was also starving, having skipped breakfast. He figured that it had to be close to noon because the sun was almost directly overhead. He really wanted to find some kind of food, even if it was some of the hard tack crackers that he fed the wounded soldiers.

"Yeah. I'm hungry, too," Darrell answered.

Private Morris led Darrell to a cluster of six or seven soldiers standing around talking.

"Hey, Sean!" Private Morris yelled to one of the soldiers. "I haven't seen you in a long time."

"Well, I'll be," the soldier said. "Jimmy Morris, is that you? I guess now that you're in the ambulance corps you're too good to talk to us common soldiers."

"Cut that out," Private Morris said. "I'm like you—I go where I'm ordered to go. I can't help it that you're never around the fighting."

The two soldiers laughed and shook hands.

"Hey, Sean, I want you to meet my partner. Darrell Stouffer, this is my best friend in the world, Private Sean McGregor."

"Hi, Private McGregor," Darrell said. He wanted to address soldiers by their rank, not by their first names.

"Sean, where can I find something to eat?" Private Morris asked.

"I don't know," Private McGregor answered. "We're looking around for food ourselves. Why don't you two join us?"

"Sean and I grew up close to each other back in Michigan," Private Morris said to Darrell. "We were best buddies in school."

"Yeah, and after the war, Jimmy and I are gonna to go to college together, and then practice law side by side," Private McGregor added. "But before we went to college, we both decided to join the army. We'd still be fighting next to each other if Jimmy hadn't got transferred."

"You ought to be glad that I did. When you go down in battle, I'll be the one that'll save your life," Private Morris said jokingly.

The soldiers walked around the large, flat, open area directly behind the soldiers who were stationed along the defensive wall. They searched a couple of places, but had no luck finding something to eat. One of the soldiers in their party ran ahead of the group and found a stash of rations. He yelled to the others to hurry and catch up before other soldiers discovered the food. Those were the last words he was to utter.

Suddenly, a large number of blasts could be heard from the Confederate lines, and the air was filled with cannonballs. When they hit, the explosions tore up everything around them, including the soldier who had left Darrell's group. The soldiers hit the ground, and Private Morris threw himself on top of Darrell to protect him from the flying shrapnel.

"What's happening?" Darrell cried. He had never witnessed anything so frightening.

"The rebs are firing their cannons at us!" Private Morris yelled to be heard above the explosions. "Darrell, we've gotta get out of here. We'll die for sure if we stay."

Private Morris dragged Darrell to his feet. The other soldiers in Darrell's group also got up and ran. The Confederate cannons kept firing. Explosions tore up the ground all around where Darrell and Private Morris were running. Then a blast came close to the two, and Private Morris threw Darrell back on the ground and landed on top of him again.

"I don't wanna die," Darrell cried as Private Morris lay on top of him. Then he remembered the last time he heard those words—when he and Kenny tried to help the wounded soldier on the first day of the battle.

"We gotta keep moving," Private Morris said as they got back to their feet.

The two ran as fast as they could away from the explosions. They finally reached a point where they were out of range of the Confederate cannons. They turned to look at the ground that they had just covered. The ground was all torn up where the shells had hit. Soldiers were lying everywhere; some were injured, but most were dead.

"I've never seen so many cannons fired at one area all at once," Private Morris said.

"I wanna leave," Darrell told him. "Can't we go back to the field hospital?"

"No. When the firing stops, we're gonna have a lot of soldiers to help. I know it's scary, but we have to stay."

The cannons kept firing. The blasts kept destroying everything in front of Darrell.

"You know, they're shooting off a lot of guns, but I don't think they're doing a lot of damage," Private Morris said.

"What do you mean? Look ahead of us. There's destruction everywhere."

"Yeah, but I think their guns are supposed to be knocking off our soldiers on the front line. The rebs are shooting over their heads. Look, Darrell."

Darrell saw that Private Morris was right. The large area where he and the small group of soldiers had been scrounging for food was being riddled with cannonballs, but where the large collection of soldiers were placed along the stone wall, there were no cannon blasts. The Confederates were overshooting their target. The soldiers all huddled on the ground as the enemy fire fell behind them.

"Look over there!" Darrell exclaimed. "What's that guy doing on a horse?"

Darrell saw a soldier on a horse riding up and down the Union lines. Artillery shells were just missing him as he rode back and forth.

"I don't know," Private Morris answered. "He's gonna get his foolish self killed though."

Private Morris looked behind him. His ambulance was a little too close to the action.

"You stay here," he said to Darrell. "I'm going to move our ambulance farther back to make sure Nellie doesn't get so upset at the cannon fire that she gets loose from her reins and runs away. Now, remember, stay down!"

"Don't leave me!" Darrell cried.

"You'll be all right here," Private Morris said. "I'll be right back." With that, Private Morris ran back to his ambulance.

Right after Private Morris left, Union cannons started firing on the Confederate guns. The air was now filled with cannon balls going each way. Darrell wasn't very far from a group of Union cannons.

The noise from their firing was deafening. Darrell lay down on the ground, covering his ears.

When the rebel cannons were being bombarded by Union artillery, they turned some of their guns and started firing in that direction. Now Darrell's spot wasn't safe anymore. Cannon balls were exploding everywhere around him again.

"Darrell, you gotta get out of there!" Private Morris screamed from behind him. "I'll tell you when to get up and run. When I do, get to your feet and get out of there as fast as you can!" He waited for a round of cannon fire to end and then screamed for Darrell to run.

Darrell got to his feet and ran as fast as he could to where Private Morris and Nellie were standing. The explosions scorched the earth behind him, and when he finally reached Private Morris, he ran right into his arms.

"It's okay, Darrell. You're gonna be okay here."

Tears of horror filled Darrell's eyes. The barrage continued behind him. The air was filled with choking smoke from the cannon fire. The land was torn apart by the incoming shells.

For over an hour the two sides fired upon each other. Every explosion frightened Darrell, even though he was safely out of range of the Confederate artillery. The Union cannons that were close to where Darrell had run away from suddenly stopped firing. Some of the guns were removed from the hill that they had fired from.

"Why aren't they firing at the rebels anymore?" Darrell asked Private Morris.

"I don't know. Maybe they ran out of ammunition. A couple of the cannons looked like they got hit by enemy fire. Maybe they can't shoot anymore."

Not long after the Union army stopped firing, the Confederate cannons stopped their bombardment, too.

"You hear that?" Private Morris asked.

"Hear what? I don't hear anything," Darrell answered.

"Exactly. The rebs have stopped firing at us. It's time to get to work."

Private Morris and Darrell climbed into the ambulance and headed to where the wounded soldiers were sprawled all over the ground. Their injuries were horrendous.

Most of the soldiers who were hit by the flying fragments were dead or close to it. Darrell turned his eyes so that he couldn't see the worst of them. Private Morris saw a soldier bleeding from a chest wound and stopped the ambulance.

"We have to hurry and get this one back to the field hospital," he told Darrell. "If we don't, I don't think he'll live for very long. Help that soldier over there with a leg wound, and I'll get this one into the ambulance."

Darrell ran over to the soldier that Private Morris had pointed to. He was bleeding from a wound just above the knee.

"You're gonna be okay," he said as he tied a tourniquet above the wound. "Hang in there. We'll get you to a doctor real fast."

Then Darrell and Private Morris went to look for another wounded soldier to help. They were both shocked to see Private Sean McGregor lying on the ground with an injured leg.

"Sean, are you okay?" Private Morris asked as he ran over to his friend.

"Yeah," Private McGregor said.

Private Morris looked at the wound. It was bad, but not as bad as the soldiers that were already in his ambulance.

"Sean, you're gonna be all right," Private Morris said to his friend. "Your wound isn't that bad. I gotta hurry and get these soldiers back to the field hospital. I'll be right back for you."

"Don't worry about me," Private McGregor said. "Save those boys' lives first."

"Sean, I'm gonna leave Darrell here with you," Private Morris said. "Darrell, bandage up Sean's wound for me."

"Sure thing, Private Morris," Darrell said.

"I'll be back as soon as I can," Private Morris said, and then he was off with the ambulance.

"I got to tear back some of your pants leg to get at the wound," Darrell told Private McGregor. "It might hurt some."

Darrell tore Private McGregor's uniform and began to wrap a bandage around the wound.

"I've seen plenty of wounds worse than this one over the past two days," Darrell said. "I think you're gonna be okay."

"I hope I can keep my leg," Private McGregor said.

"The doctors will do everything they can to save it," Darrell said reassuringly.

After he was done bandaging the wound, the two of them sat back, looking over the bombed area. The moaning of other wounded soldiers could be heard. Darrell saw the same man riding on his horse that he had seen during the bombardment.

"We saw that guy riding up and down the line while the cannons were firing all around," Darrell said to Private McGregor. "What was he doing out there?"

"That's General Hancock. I bet he was trying to keep his soldiers calm by riding among them during the shooting."

"But he could've been killed," Darrell said, questioning the officer's logic.

"That's Hancock for you. He cares more about his soldiers than he does his own life. That's why his men love him so much."

"I'm glad all of the firing stopped," Darrell said. "I couldn't take much more of the noise of cannonballs exploding. You think that the rebs are done for the day?"

"Done?" Private McGregor said. "They haven't hardly started yet. When one side shoots off a lot of cannons like the rebels just did, it is usually the sign that the infantry is gonna attack. I'm guessing that General Lee is gonna send his army at us pretty soon."

Darrell thought about Private McGregor's prediction. He hoped that he was wrong, but he figured that the soldier knew what he was talking about. Darrell braced himself to watch another Confederate attack. Would it be as desperate as the attack on Little Round Top? He hoped that he would see the Union army finally defeat Lee's army and send them back to Virginia. Waiting for the rebels to attack was hard for Darrell. But he didn't have to wait very long.

# Chapter 17

## THE CONFEDERATE ATTACK

Darrell and Private McGregor were sitting on the ground three hundred yards back from the front line of the Union defenses. The soldiers who were previously lying on the ground during the Confederate cannonade were now up, readying for an enemy attack.

Between Darrell and Private McGregor, in the open area where the majority of the rebel shells hit, were numerous wounded and dead soldiers.

In front of the Union stone wall, there was a large, unplanted farm field that was at least a half of a mile long. Beyond the flat field was a thickly wooded forest. Darrell looked, but he couldn't find the Confederate soldiers that would be attacking.

"Where do you think the rebs are?" he asked Private McGregor.

"Look, here they come," Private McGregor answered.

Out of the forest came the rebel soldiers. Darrell could scarcely believe the number of Confederates that were emerging from the woods.

"How many soldiers do you think there are?" Darrell asked.

"Gotta be thousands," Private McGregor answered. "Maybe ten thousand or even more."

"Do we have that many soldiers on our line?"

"We probably got a little more than half of that," Private McGregor responded. "Even though they outnumber us, I wouldn't want to be one of those rebs attacking for anything."

"Why is that, Private McGregor?"

"You see that field in front of you?" Private McGregor said, pointing to the empty farm field. "Those rebs are gonna have to walk across that before they get to our lines. They got no place to hide. First our cannons will blast them, and then our rifles will fire on them. They're gonna lose a lot of men trying to make this charge."

"Do you think General Lee knows this?"

"Sure, Darrell. But he's counting on that enough of them will still be standing when they finally reach our boys. It's a big gamble. We tried it at Fredericksburg."

"Private McGregor, did you fight in that battle?" Darrell asked. "I read about it in our local newspaper."

"Yeah, but I didn't get called into the battle until near the end. So many good soldiers gave up their lives that day because General Burnside kept calling for charge after charge. We had about as much of a chance to take the rebel lines then as they have to take our lines today."

Private McGregor sounded so sure that many Confederate soldiers would lose their lives. Darrell wanted to believe him, but he couldn't help but think that a general who was as smart as Lee was wouldn't be willing to send his troops into a slaughter.

Darrell watched more and more Confederates soldiers come out of the woods and line up in front of it. The rebel army stretched out in lines that ran across for almost a mile. The regiments that made up the assaulting army were three to four lines deep. Each regiment's flag proudly waved in the breeze. The soldiers stood shoulder to shoulder as each regiment gathered. It was an impressive display of military might.

The order was given, and the mighty force of the Southern army began marching toward the Union lines. The Northern soldiers watched them begin their assault. The rebels were too far out of range of their rifles. Reinforcements strengthened the Union lines. With such a big force coming at it, where to place the Northern soldiers wasn't hard to figure out.

"The way that they're marching forward is almost like a parade," Darrell said admiringly. "They look so great marching together like they are."

"It sure is a sight," Private McGregor said. "Keep your head down, Darrell. Our cannons are probably gonna open fire soon."

Just as Private McGregor predicted, the Union cannons opened fire. Shell after shell was sent hurtling at the great accumulation of rebel soldiers. You didn't have to have perfect aim. You simply had to fire toward the big blob of gray figures, and you were bound to hit something. Explosions sent Confederate soldiers flying into the air. The rebels were packed so close together that one cannon ball could take out as many as ten men.

Darrell watched as the Union cannons shredded the Confederate lines. What he once thought was a grand spectacle was turning into an ugly mass of dead and wounded bodies.

"The cannons don't seem to stop the rebs from coming," he said to Private McGregor. "When some of them go down, others from behind run up to take their place."

"I told you that they'd lose a lot of men," Private McGregor said. "And we just started firing into them. The rebels still have a long way to go to reach our lines."

"Do you think the soldiers knew before they started that many would die?" Darrell asked.

"They knew."

"Then why did they start walking across that field? Why didn't they say that they wouldn't do it?" Darrell questioned, wanting to know how soldiers could walk to their death so calmly.

"Soldiers follow orders. You don't question them. Once the firing starts, you carry out the orders, not from a sense of duty, but because you don't want to let down the other soldiers around you."

The Union cannons kept firing, and the Confederate soldiers kept falling. Hundreds of rebels were littered over the ground. The army kept moving forward.

The Confederates came to a road that was about halfway between the woods where they had started and the Union defensive lines. Before they could cross the road, the soldiers had to climb over a wooden fence that ran all along the side of the road. This fence slowed the momentum of the Confederate march. The soldiers began to pile up, waiting for those in front of them to get over the fence. The cannon fire became more deadly, if that was possible. The gigantic congestion of soldiers made it even easier for Northern shells to score direct hits. Hundreds of soldiers died waiting to climb over the fence.

A noise from behind Darrell and Private McGregor signaled the return of Private Morris. He had left his ambulance away from the fighting to protect his horse.

"Private Morris, it's terrible," Darrell said.

"Terrible?" Private McGregor responded. "We're winning the battle. We're knocking out a lot of them rebels. How can that be terrible?"

"I'm sorry, Private McGregor," Darrell apologized. "I just have a hard time seeing so many men die all at once."

"He didn't mean anything by it," Private Morris told his friend.

"I know," Private McGregor said. "It's just that we've taken a beating so often from General Lee that it's good to see our boys give it to him for a change."

As the Confederate soldiers crossed the road, they were now in range of the Union rifles. All at once, a huge mass of blue uniforms rose up from behind their defenses, leveled their rifles, and shot into the gray mass of enemy soldiers. Hundreds of rebel fighting men dropped all at once. As easy as it was for the Union cannons to score hits, it was that easy for the Northern rifles to bring down Confederate soldiers. They just had to fire their guns into the crowd of enemy soldiers, and they were bound to hit a rebel. *This isn't war*, Darrell thought. *This is slaughter.*

The rebel soldiers kept advancing. They were condensing their big line of soldiers, aiming at the middle of the Union defenses. They were firing back at the Northern soldiers, many of whom were now falling.

"They've lost so many men," Darrell said. "Do you think that they'll ever reach our lines?"

"I don't know," Private McGregor replied. "I didn't think so when they first started across that field, but they still have lots of soldiers advancing, and they're getting close to our soldiers."

"They're still losing a lot of men for every inch of ground they gain," Private Morris said.

Darrell saw a Confederate general take off his hat. He took his sword, stuck it through the hat, and waved to his soldiers. A large group of Confederates ran with the general toward the Union lines. The first bunch of rebels running ahead were all shot down by Union infantry fire. But the soldiers behind them made it over the Union defenses.

"Where's my rifle," Private McGregor asked. "I got to get down there and help out."

"You aren't going anywhere with that leg wound," Private Morris said to him.

"If you help me to my feet, I think I can make it down there. That's my regiment. I need to help them out."

"Sean, there's no way you can walk down there. You couldn't take two steps without falling over," Private Morris said.

"I can't just sit here and watch," Private McGregor called out.

Where the Confederates had broken through the defenses, their soldiers and the Union soldiers were locked in hand-to-hand combat. Darrell was concerned, as he saw more enemy soldiers flood through the hole in the Northern position. The rebel general who had urged his men forward was with some of his comrades, trying to turn a Union cannon around. He was going to take the gun that had brought down so many of his men and use it to bring down some of the Union soldiers for a change.

"Look, Private McGregor!" Darrell cried. "Here come some reinforcements!"

A large group of Union soldiers were running to help those who were fighting the Confederates. They crashed into the rebels who had broken through the lines. The tide of the battle turned, and the Union soldiers were taking the fight to the rebels. In a matter of minutes, the Southern soldiers who didn't surrender were shot down. The Northern defensive position held. The assault was over. It had been a tremendous disaster for the South. Darrell saw the Confederate general, who had urged his men forward and looked like he would bring victory to his side, lying dead next to the cannon that he had tried to turn around.

"We stopped them!" yelled Private McGregor. "We beat old Bobby Lee's army!"

"What are the soldiers on the front line yelling?" Private Morris asked.

"They're yelling '*Fredericksburg!*'" Private McGregor replied. "We finally paid the rebels back for the beating we took at Fredericksburg!"

Darrell was happy that the Union army had won, but he did not feel like celebrating. He had hoped to see General Lee take a whooping. Looking over the battlefield, littered with soldiers, he realized that he had gotten what he had come to see. The only thing was that he had watched too many brave men sacrifice their lives trying to carry out General Lee's orders. There were so many of them lying on the ground. How could he celebrate? The Confederates had paid too big a price for the Union's victory.

The Confederate soldiers limped back across the big farm field. Some Union soldiers kept firing at them, but most had stopped to enjoy their victory. Some of the rebel soldiers reached down and tried to help some of the wounded walk back with them. *It's a sad sight*, Darrell thought.

"Come on, Darrell," Private Morris said. "Let's get Sean into the ambulance and begin helping other soldiers down there. We've got a lot of men to run back to the field hospital."

"You stay here with your friend, and I'll run and get Nellie," Darrell volunteered.

Darrell raced back and got the ambulance. He brought it down to where Private Morris and Private McGregor were. It was going to be a long afternoon, helping all of the wounded soldiers. Other ambulances had also arrived to transport injured soldiers.

After putting Private McGregor in the ambulance, Darrell and Private Morris worked on another wounded soldier.

"Private Morris, if we get done helping our soldiers, do you think we can help some of the rebels?" Darrell asked.

"We have a lot of help with the other ambulance crews around, but we also have a lot of our soldiers to attend to. Maybe after we get all of our boys back to the surgeons, there will be enough light left to help some of the rebs," Private Morris answered.

"You know, I ran away from home to fight in the war," Darrell told Private Morris. "After watching the fighting over the last three days, I don't think I ever wanna see a war again."

"I know what you mean," Private Morris said. "These three days at Gettysburg are the bloodiest I've ever seen. I hope I don't ever see anything like it again."

The two loaded the injured soldier into the ambulance and sped off to the field hospital.

# Chapter 18

# THE SOLUTION

Darrell and Private Morris worked until sunset, helping the wounded soldiers. There had been so many Union soldiers that needed medical care that neither Darrell and Private Morris nor any of the other ambulance crews had time to start helping the Confederate wounded. They still lay on the battlefield, crying out in pain from their injuries. It was hard leaving so many bodies on the battlefield at the end of the day. Darrell felt bad that he hadn't been able to help any of the brave rebel soldiers who had marched across the open field.

When he made his way into the town of Gettysburg, he found out that the Confederate army was no longer there. Darrell remembered what Private Morris had told him earlier that day: "When General Lee pulls his army out of Gettysburg, then you'll know that the battle is over." He was glad the battle was over. He had seen too many soldiers die during the past three days.

The citizens from the town who had been imprisoned in their houses during the battle were now exercising their freedom, walking around the streets. A gentle rain was falling, finally breaking up the humidity that had gripped the area over the past few days, but the people of Gettysburg didn't seem to mind the shower as they congregated outside. They were just happy to be out of their houses.

When Darrell returned to the McElroy's, he found a bunch of people had gathered next door at the Johnson residence. Mr.

Johnson was holding court, talking to the small crowd that had gathered there.

*He sure loves to talk,* Darrell said to himself as he saw the assemblage. Uncle Levi noticed Darrell as he was walking up the path to his house. He left Mr. Johnson's oration to go and talk with Darrell.

"What's Mr. Johnson talking about over there?" Darrell asked Uncle Levi.

"He was telling everyone about the Wade family. They had a daughter, Jennie. I guess Jennie was baking bread for the soldiers today when a bullet crashed into her house and killed her."

"That's so sad," Darrell responded.

"I feel bad for the Wade family, but I think she was the only resident from town who died in the three days of battle. The way that bullets were flying through town the past few days, it's no wonder that more people didn't get hurt. Anyway, c'mon inside. The girls have been cooking up a storm since the rebels left town. Supper should be just about ready."

Darrell and Uncle Levi went inside and sat down for dinner. Elizabeth and Aunt Clara had indeed been cooking since the Confederates moved out of town, and the four sat down to a table abundant with food. They hadn't eaten like this since the dinner on Tuesday evening when Darrell and Kenny first showed up. Darrell told the McElroys about the cannon barrage that preceded the rebel attack.

"We were so scared," Aunt Clara commented as Darrell talked about the cannon bombardment. "The whole house was shaking. We were down in the basement, but we were afraid that the house would collapse in on us, it was rattling so much!"

"I knew that there'd be an attack after all of that cannon fire," Uncle Levi added. "I just wasn't sure who would be attacking who. When the rebels left town, I knew that whatever had happened, they had lost. So you say the Confederates attacked our boys?"

"Yeah," Darrell said, with a heavy heart. "They walked across this big field only to be slaughtered by our army."

"Well, you came to Gettysburg hoping to see General Lee take a beating. Was it everything that you thought it would be?" Uncle Levi asked.

"I thought that seeing Bobby Lee getting whooped would be the greatest sight in my life. But I saw those rebel boys go down in such great numbers that it was impossible for me to be happy."

"So does this mean you'll be leaving tomorrow to go back home?" Uncle Levi questioned.

"There's still a lot of wounded on the battlefield. Some of them have been lying there since Wednesday. If it's okay with you, I'd like to stay a few more days and help out where I can," Darrell responded.

"Sleep in tomorrow and wait for me," Uncle Levi said. "We'll go back to the Union lines together. There's probably a whole lot to do to get this place back to normal again."

"Mr. McElroy, I bet it'll take months before this place is normal. Maybe it'll never go back to the way it was. There are so many wounded soldiers. I don't know where they can all go to get better attention."

"Maybe we can help with that," Uncle Levi said. "We got lots of room here. We can take in a couple of soldiers. I owe the army that after having served in it."

"What about the dead soldiers?" Aunt Clara replied. "They're gonna need a proper burial."

"I'll tell you what," Uncle Levi suggested. "Before we go up to the battlefield tomorrow, we'll stop by my store to see what's left of it. I used to have a bunch of shovels. If I still have some, we'll bring them with us to help dig graves."

"Okay, but I want to go back to the field hospital and help out there," Darrell said.

"All right. But on Sunday, I'm gonna hitch my horse to the wagon, and we're gonna ride back to Dubaville," Uncle Levi insisted. "You need to show your folks that you're all right. If you come back here with me later on in the day, it's gotta be with your parents' permission."

"I hope that they'll let me come back," Darrell said. "I've gotten to like helping wounded soldiers. I hope that I'll still be able to keep doing it."

The four sat around the table for the next few hours. Darrell described the Confederate charge as the three McElroys listened intently. Then he dragged himself up to bed. It had been another exhausting day. Darrell sat on the edge of the bed, hoping that Elizabeth would make her nightly visit. A knock on the door alerted him to her presence.

"Hi, Darrell," she said as she came into the room.

"Hi, Elizabeth. I was hoping that you would stop by tonight," Darrell replied.

"I'm so glad that you'll be staying with us a few extra days."

"Yeah, and if my mother and father say it's okay, I can come back and help out some more."

"Do you think that you'll be in trouble when you get home?" Elizabeth asked.

"I'm always in trouble," Darrell replied. "Especially with a brother like Jeremiah. I'm used to it, though. I just hope I'm not in so much trouble that they'll make me stay at home and say I can't come back to Gettysburg."

"Do you think I can go with you and my father to the battlefield tomorrow?"

"Elizabeth, I don't think you should see some of the things that are up there. It'd be better if you and your mother stayed home and cooked for the wounded soldiers. If your dad takes in a couple of them, the sight of their wounds will probably be hard enough to look at."

"Dad said that Mr. Redunski took in some of the wounded. He said that they bled all over their new carpet. When the soldiers finally leave, they'll have to throw it out because there's so much blood ground into it. I wonder if that'll happen to us, too."

"Probably," Darrell sympathized. "But remember, these soldiers fought bravely over the past few days. Take good care of them."

"I will, but I'm not so good at the sight of blood," Elizabeth said, cringing with fear.

"I had a hard time at first, seeing the wounds and the blood," Darrell responded. "I just kept looking at the soldiers' faces. That helped me a lot."

"Darrell, do you think the rebels will head back to Virginia tomorrow?"

"Probably," Darrell answered. "I couldn't celebrate the Union victory after watching so many rebs die, but I'll be happy to see Bobby Lee heading south. I don't think he'll be in a hurry to attack Pennsylvania again."

"Well, I better let you get some rest," Elizabeth suggested.

"Wait, Elizabeth," Darrell hastened to say. "I want to ask your opinion on something. It's been eating at me all day."

"Sure, what is it?"

"You see, this morning I was out helping wounded soldiers when this doctor, Captain Robinson, told me that he thought that I would make a good doctor. He said that he'd even pay for my college."

"That's great, Darrell."

"Hold on, Elizabeth. Here's my problem," Darrell said sadly.

He then proceeded to tell Elizabeth about the pranks he had pulled in school, especially the last one with the snakes. Then he told her about how Mrs. Garber told him he couldn't go back to school.

"If I can't go back to school, I don't know if I can learn enough to pass that college test," Darrell lamented.

"You and Kenny were just having fun," Elizabeth said. "You were just being kids. It's too bad that your teacher couldn't see that."

"Yeah, but we sort of took it too far," Darrell owned up. "That was my fault. I never thought that playing around in school would screw things up for me later in life."

"Well, maybe I have a solution to your problem," Elizabeth said.

"What is it? I'll do anything," Darrell said hopefully.

"Maybe you could go to school here. We have a good school in town, and our teacher, Mr. Morehouse, is the best. We have a college in town called Gettysburg College. Lots of students who

Mr. Morehouse has taught have gone on to school there. They have an entrance exam, too, and I haven't heard of anyone who applied there failing the test. He must be good at preparing students to take it. He could help you get ready for college."

"Elizabeth, that's a great idea. But do you think your dad would let me stay here when I go to school?"

"Yeah. Darrell, he really likes you. And Darrell, he'll never admit it, but he needs some help with his store. It's getting too big for him to run it by himself. Maybe you could help him after school every day. I'm sure he'd let you stay here in exchange for helping him."

"And if I got to stay here, I'd be able to see you all of the time," Darrell said. "I'd like that."

"Me too," Elizabeth said, and she turned beet red from embarrassment. Expressions of love were new to both Darrell and Elizabeth.

"Elizabeth, I think you just saved me. I could even go home on weekends to help my father run the farm and return on Sunday nights to be ready for another week of school."

"We can talk more about this with my parents in the morning," Elizabeth said. "I should probably be getting back to my room now."

Darrell walked Elizabeth to the door, holding her hand. She turned to him as they reached the door, and she turned red from her shyness. Darrell looked into her eyes, smiled, and then kissed her quickly. Then she was gone again, leaving him with just mental images of her beauty.

Darrell went back to his bed and lay down. He thought about everything that had happened over the past few days. It seemed like years since he and Kenny had run away from home. He felt different now from when he left Dubaville—more grown-up. He had started this journey hoping be a hero and to watch General Lee lose. He was no hero, but he had seen Lee take a beating. And now, he had found a future. He was going to be a doctor, and he had the love of a pretty girl to help him.

Darrell stuck his hand in his pocket and pulled out the patch that Captain Robinson had given him earlier in the day. He ran his fingers along the caduceus that was sewn into the patch. Then he stopped and took a good look at the Greek symbol.

"Snakes," he said to himself, smiling. "There are two snakes on this symbol."

Darrell thought back to May when he sneaked the two snakes into school and completely disrupted Mrs. Garber's class. Those snakes were a part of the old Darrell Stouffer. Those snakes had helped to take away his education and introduce him to a life as a farmer—a life he wasn't sure he really wanted.

He looked at the caduceus again. These two snakes, he decided, were a symbol of the new Darrell. These snakes brought back his chance at going to school. They brought hope that one day he would have a life that he truly wanted—one as a doctor.

Darrell decided that if he made it through college he would become a military doctor just like Captain Robinson. He would help the brave soldiers who fought in future wars. He could never be the hero in battle that he had earlier dreamed of being.

"It is the real soldiers," Darrell said to himself, "who are the true heroes of war."